JUST FOR YOU

YASH PATEL

INDIA • SINGAPORE • MALAYSIA

Notion Press

Old No. 38, New No. 6
McNichols Road, Chetpet
Chennai - 600 031

First Published by Notion Press 2019
Copyright © Yash Patel 2019
All Rights Reserved.

ISBN 978-1-64678-812-5

This book has been published with all efforts taken to make the material error-free after the consent of the author. However, the author and the publisher do not assume and hereby disclaim any liability to any party for any loss, damage, or disruption caused by errors or omissions, whether such errors or omissions result from negligence, accident, or any other cause.

While every effort has been made to avoid any mistake or omission, this publication is being sold on the condition and understanding that neither the author nor the publishers or printers would be liable in any manner to any person by reason of any mistake or omission in this publication or for any action taken or omitted to be taken or advice rendered or accepted on the basis of this work. For any defect in printing or binding the publishers will be liable only to replace the defective copy by another copy of this work then available.

For my wife, Jaishree, my rock and my guiding light.

Contents

Acknowledgements	7
The Preface	9
The Prologue	11
1. The Sunrise	13
2. The Baseball Cap	21
3. The Ice Cream	26
4. The Pretty Hair	28
5. The Present	31
6. The Preparation	34
7. The Movie Star	37
8. The Dress	38
9. The Eggs	40
10. The Swami	42
11. The Serving Dish	46
12. The Seagull	52
13. The Gift	54
14. The Fragrance	58
15. The Coy	60
16. The Marker	62
17. The Glasses	64
18. The Passion	70
19. The Nightcap	77
20. The Bonfire	80
21. The Paan	82
22. The Internet	84
23. The Son	88
24. The Coffee	90
25. The Cable	93
26. The Dress	95
27. The Uncle	99
28. The Golden Ganesh	102
29. The Duchess	106
30. The Bass	113
31. The Stars and the Moon	114

Contents

32. The Arcade	118
33. The Window	128
34. The Milk	130
35. The Swallows	132
36. The Big File	135
37. The Valet	137
38. The Club	140
39. The Afternoon Nap	143
40. The Last Laugh	147
41. The Marlin	151
42. The Sacrifice	153
43. The Madras Coffee	157
44. The Hug	159
45. The Pearl	162
46. The Crashing Chair	166
47. The Eggplant	173
48. The Thunder	176
49. The Beach House	179
50. The Cat	181
51. The Pitch	185
52. The Envelope	186
53. The Phone Call	189
54. The Wakeup Call	191
55. The Dancing Crows	193
56. The Compromise	196
57. The Wall	199
58. The Sindoor	202
59. The Stray	207
60. The Patient	210
61. The Zap	211
62. The Vermillion	213
63. The Mourning After	218
64. The Salute	219
65. The Tip	220
66. The White Kurta	223
67. The Body	230
68. The News	232
69. The Snack	234
The Epilogue	*245*

Acknowledgements

I want to start by thanking my son, Trishul. From reviewing early drafts to helping craft essential passages to editing the final manuscript, his commitment and direction were essential in completing this story. Thank you, son.

I also want to thank everyone on the Notion Press team, who helped bring this novel across the finish line. It was an experience I will never forget, and one that I could not have accomplished without the astute guidance of such steadfast and talented individuals.

The Preface

This is a work of fiction. The names, characters, businesses, places, and events are either the products of the author's imagination or used in a fictitious manner. Any resemblance to any actual person is coincidental.

No, this story is not written about somebody in particular. Instead, this tale reflects upon everyday experiences that we all share. From getting dressed to driving to work, to having lunch, to having a few drinks, to having dinner. All these experiences define our lives. But woven into these everyday happenings are the impressions of someone else. A someone that we not only seek comfort from but also seek to comfort. And it is this someone that is always on our mind because it is this someone that is always in our heart. Thus, the things that we do, we do because of and for this special someone.

Yes, this is a love story, but of a different kind. Love is difficult to define. It is a connection that is as strong as steel. But it is ethereal as well. Like water, it can pass through a sieve, without notice. But it can also carve a valley in one's soul as deep as a canyon. And sometimes, love persists, no matter how hard one tries to forget and move on.

This is the story of a man who possesses everything in life. Yet, he still believes in simplicity, and he cares for his fellow human beings. This man believes in one guiding principle: Born as a human. Live like a human. Die as a human.

The Prologue

It is late evening. Two young adults, older than boys but not quite men, swim in the ocean. One is larger and more muscular than the other. However, both appear to be of about the same age.

Enough clouds fill the air to provide cover for the moon and most of the city, which hides behind the now almost empty beach. The evening sky is navy blue from above, but near the horizon, it transitions to hues of purple, orange, and red. The sunset paints the vivid sky these dark colours far out beyond the shipping vessels that scatter the bay.

The tired sun begins to disappear for the day. And as it does, its rays begin to drape the cold ocean surface with a shimmer of excitement and energy. A lofty breeze adds to the ocean's choppiness. It is high tide, and darkness begins to take over.

The two youths decide to race out to the buoy beyond the farthest visible sailboat. They want to take one final lap before calling it a day. And as the sun goes down, the tide picks up, and a storm begins to gather. Dark and heavy clouds from the north bring in colder air. A wall of rain marches south.

Both swimmers keep pace with each other as they make their way farther out to sea. The more muscular swimmer has bursts of energy every now and then, yet his muscles strain to keep going. Soon, he ends up tailing his friend,

The Prologue

who makes a steady pace towards the buoy in the distance. Both are exhausted, but neither stops to rest.

The storm can no longer go unnoticed. It begins to rage. It demands attention. But neither swimmer notices. After passing the midpoint, the larger male, with tired arms and lungs out of breath, begins to fall behind his friend. Still, neither stops to rest. Soon after this, the larger one is caught in a rip current. And he struggles, even more, to keep up.

After much exertion, the larger of the two goes under the water. The smaller swimmer, as if compelled to look back at the right moment, notices that his friend is gone. Without hesitation, he dives under to save his friend. Both disappear under the waves for some time. Bubbles reach the surface. But the vast ocean feigns indifference, and the storm is now hostile and full of contempt.

Then finally, the skinny swimmer manages to pull the larger one's head above the water. Both gasp, but not enough to take a full breath of air. Before either can take another breath, both go under again. Once again, the vast ocean feigns indifference. On the surface, the waves are resentful and angry, but from far above, the sea appears to sparkle and glisten with delight.

More bubbles reach the surface, but for some time, nothing else is noticeable as compared to the incessant turmoil of the crashing waves. Then after what seems like too long, both bodies surge upward from the water. The skinnier one propels the more muscular friend towards the heavens as the two resurface. The two swimmers are gasping, coughing, and out of breath. Yet, it soon becomes clear that they both will survive the ordeal.

The Sunrise

This tale revolves around many characters. They all have different professions, passions, and lifestyles. The story takes place in New Mumbai, a suburb of the Indian metropolis with the same name. And it begins in the home of the well-to-do Malhotra family.

Prakash is the patriarch. He is well known by friends and acquaintances alike for being jovial and boisterous. He is a well-established surgeon who has been practising medicine for decades at the same hospital. He is tall and large, with broad shoulders, and a heavy-set waist. His head is significant, and he has a pleasant yet commanding countenance. The physician is proud of his place in life and of his profession. But most of all, he is proud of his family, which includes his wife, Meena, and his only daughter, Anika.

The family's lavish lifestyle is evident from its large house located in the heart of New Mumbai. The five-bedroom mansion, with a pool house (but no pool) and a four-car garage, is not palatial. Rather, it is traditional in design and architecture. The home has three stories, with two balconies in the front that face the courtyard. A rooftop terrace overlooks the backyard. And a ten-foot concrete wall covered with and hidden by lush green vines surrounds the home. Creamy white and vibrant red rose bushes line the inside perimeter of the wall.

The courtyard leading up to the carport adorns a water fountain with *Lord Ganesha* at its centre. Six jets line the inside of the basin, shooting water over three meters into the air. Coloured lights surround its inside edge. Prakash had the jets and lights wired soon after moving in. Now, whenever the home's central music system plays a song, the fountain's jets and lights come to life. "Like a mini-Bellagio," as he is known to tell his guests.

Meena manages household affairs like a business. She is a loving wife and mother. But she is also particular and stern. Unlike Prakash, Meena is slim and tiny. She is also full of energy, and she never stops to rest. Her home is immaculate and orderly. Every room is custom-designed to fit her traditional taste. Every room is neat and tidy. Everything has its place, down to the smallest ornament and decoration.

She keeps tabs on all matters relating to the family friends and relatives. She always remembers to wish everyone on their birthday or anniversary. She is the first to reach out to someone in need of care or help. She tends to worry about everyone's well-being.

Most of all, Meena worries about her husband and her daughter. She wants the best for both of them, but sometimes the woman cannot help but meddle in their affairs. It's not because she wants to control every moment of their lives. Or at least, she thinks she does not. Rather, she wants to protect them from all harm, whether she can do anything about it or not.

In the past, she would often bribe her daughter's classmates with sweets. Meena always seemed to have an endless supply of *laddu*, *boondi*, *jalebi*, or some other sugary treat with her. Even if she **did not** have her purse anywhere near her, somehow, she could make a *mithai* appear out of thin air. Thus, if any classmate were to hear of anyone bad-mouthing her daughter, Meena was always the first to know.

One time, when Anika was in the sixth grade, Meena caught wind of a classmate talking down about her daughter. The girl suggested that Anika was spoiled and had poor taste in clothing. Meena found out that very day. She reported the student to the school's principal without thinking twice. She then made sure the family of the girl knew about the situation and had them called in to confront the student. She knew that she was too intrusive. But she cannot help herself, even now that Anika is all grown up. These days, Meena's main concerns are her husband's health and her daughter's career.

Even though she grew up surrounded by luxury, Anika is not spoiled. Before going to university, she spent her summers volunteering at a local orphanage. There she realized how fortunate she was to be born into a well-off family.

At first, bonding with the orphans made her feel guilty of her privileged upbringing. But soon after, Anika resolved to figure out a way to give back to society. She knew deep down that she wanted to devote her life to helping others. But she had no idea how she would do any of this. She knew in her heart that she would figure it out someday.

Her family and friends would often ask Anika about how she would fulfil her ambitions. All Anika could say in these situations was, "I just know." The young lady had a determined temperament that showed resolve but did not instil confidence. Therefore, most people did not think she was serious. "Maybe you should apply to medical school?" Prakash would tell her now and then. In response, Anika would shrug her shoulders. Granted, the medical profession is virtuous. But Anika had grander dreams. Yet, she could not admit this to anyone else but herself.

Anika had graduated from university a few months ago with a degree in Sociology. But she is yet to take the next step. Until recently, she used to spend her free time at the orphanage. But not anymore. Above all, the young lady regrets not doing more about her lofty goals. Anika is fit and athletic, and she likes to play competitive sports. But most people of her age are busy with careers and starting a family. Given this, she often ends up running alone if she can motivate herself. Of late, even this has been a challenge for her.

Yet, this a notable time for the Malhotras. Prakash is about to celebrate his fiftieth birthday. Also, today is his twenty-fifth wedding anniversary. To celebrate both events, they are planning a big party. Prakash loves to party, and Meena loves to organize them. It works out well for both. These events allow the father to unwind and get away from his stressful career. Also, they enable the mother to update herself on the latest gossip. It's a win-win.

Tradition runs deep in the Malhotra family. Each morning, Prakash, Meena, and Anika gather in the prayer room to begin the day. The tiny room is on the first floor. It is next to the living room, to the left of the staircase. It is large enough to accommodate the family, but it is cosy and comforting. A wooden aedicule separates the deities from the worshippers, and a *diya* is lit and set before the gods.

Early this particular morning, the daughter sits at her desk in front of her diary. She rubs her elbows as if they are itching at the same time. And on the open page, Anika has created the following list:

Master Plan (for today)

1. Read more (ask Sughandha).
2. ~~Apologize to~~ Find new orphanage.
3. Exercise (jog, ~~perhaps~~).

Lately, she has been struggling to motivate herself. So, instead of writing in her diary, she decided to come up with a list of items that she wants to accomplish for the day. "Baby steps," as her mother used to say when she was young. Anika begins to read out her list to herself while looking into her eyes in the mirror.

As she does this, Meena calls out, "Wake up, sleepyhead!"

"Coming, Mommy!" Anika shouts from her bedroom. Anika's brain is wide awake, but her body feels exhausted. The young lady has been up for some time, as she could not sleep again. In fact, it has been a while since she had a good night's rest. Last night, she felt more restless than ever.

"Young lady!" Meena yells towards the ceiling. "Honestly, what is up with our little girl these days?"

"She's not little anymore, Meena. She just needs discipline. Plain and simple!" Prakash grumbles. He is often stern, but more so before his morning coffee.

The daughter pokes her head into the prayer room and chortles, "Maybe I'll join the Army. Oooh, or how about the Navy? I've always wanted to travel. And this way, I can see the world from a boat. It will be like a perpetual cruise. Can you imagine it? Captain Anika. Wow!"

"You won't last one day, Anika. Every day, it's something new with you." The mother gives a doubtful expression as if the daughter is serious.

"At least we won't have to lend her more money for food and clothes. She'll get three meals a day and a free uniform. I'll take you to the recruitment office right after lunch."

"Prakash, don't encourage her!" the mother scolds the father.

"Don't worry, Mommy. I won't disappear so easily. I still need to pack my bags and clean my room. That could take days." Both father and daughter are smirking at this point, but Meena is not amused.

"Can we get started already? I have too much work to do today than to listen to you two crack jokes." The mother feels exasperated and wants to get going with her morning routine.

Once they settle themselves, they begin with a small prayer. And today, the husband and wife wish each other well on their anniversary.

During the morning prayer, Prakash turns to the daughter. "Remember that my old friend, Raj, will be at the railway station this morning. So please don't be late." Facing Meena, he continues. "It's been twenty-five years. Do you recall how close we were?"

"I remember very well," Meena admits. "You were inseparable. Didn't he graduate with you?"

"No, he just hung out on campus, pretending to be a medical student. Raj wasn't even a student."

"Wow! Are you serious?" Anika asks with intrigue.

"I never knew that," Meena adds, with a perplexed look on her face.

"When was the last time you saw each other?" Anika inquires.

"On our wedding day," Prakash responds after a short pause. "Afterwards, I went overseas for my surgery training. Raj went back to Goa to help take care of his ailing father. I didn't hear from him since, until last week."

Anika's eyes widen.

"Daddy found him on Facebook," Meena explains.

Raj had discovered that his old friend was now a famous surgeon in Mumbai. And after they connected, Prakash invited Raj to his upcoming celebration.

"What does Uncle Raj look like? How will I identify him at the train station?" Anika asks her father.

"No idea," Prakash replies. "It's been so long, and he doesn't have a single picture on his Facebook profile. But knowing Raj, he'll be wearing a simple attire. Nothing fancy. I bet he doesn't even have a cellphone."

"That doesn't help. That could be anyone." Anika frowns.

The mother has an idea, "Take that photo of Daddy and Raj that's sitting on Daddy's desk in his office."

"The one of Raj and me on the beach? Better than nothing, I guess," the father agrees, and then turns to Anika, "You're a smart girl. I'm sure you'll figure it out."

"Gee. Thank you, Daddy." Anika is not amused.

The Baseball Cap

Crowds of travellers consume the station from within and spill out into the pickup area. More and more passengers empty from arriving trains, far more than seem to depart. It is still dawn, but the station is busy and lively.

Vendors of all types are all over. Some are walking with baskets under their arms or on top of their heads. Others are on the steps, selling trinkets and toys. More established vendors have booths. Those less fortunate lay their goods down on a blanket on the ground, as they sit in the middle. A young boy sells DVDs, but the packages are worn and tattered. The air is thick and stale and humid, and a fine mist of dust and particles hangs motionless in the haze. The fluorescent lights from above do little to dissolve the thick and heavy air. It is loud because of all the people, but it is also loud because of all the music. At least five different *Bollywood* songs fill the air at any one time.

Anika and her driver pull up to the pickup area.

Anika is unsure how to proceed given the unfolding chaos before her. But at the same time, she is excited and eager to find her mystery guest. She tells herself that she will go up to the first old man to come across her path. The young lady takes one last look at the picture of her father and his friend, and she jumps out of the car. Looking back, she shouts, "If I'm not back in an hour, send in a rescue team to find me." And she disappears into the mass of people.

Ramu, Prakash's driver, waits in the car. He is the family's chauffeur, secretary, and security guard. He also coordinates the family's day-to-day activities. Ramu has some unique talents. He can sing. He is great at telling jokes. He can impersonate many yesteryear *Bollywood* stars, such as Amitabh Bachchan and Sanjeev Kumar. His face always gives the impression that he is about to laugh. But he seldom does. Ramu is also a bit pudgy after indulging on Meena's endless *mithai* over the years. Yet his countenance is full and bright, and his body is healthy and of average height and build.

Whenever he drives, Ramu wears his aviator sunglasses. He always wears a dark green, military-style outfit, but nobody knows why. If you ever ask Ramu, you will get a different answer every time. "Because it was on sale." "I won it at an auction for retired generals." "It was my late father's dying wish that I wear this." Ramu was never in the military, nor was anyone from his family. None of his responses ever made any sense, and after a while, people stopped asking.

Ramu's wife, Sughandha, has her own unique traits. She is a bookworm, with no interest in her surroundings. In public and in private, she is always reading. Even during their wedding and honeymoon, all Sughandha did was read her books. At most, you'll hear Sughandha say one or two words in a conversation. And most days, all she ever says is "Yes," "No," "Fine," and "Maybe." She is the same height as Ramu, but she is slenderer. Sughandha also looks older than Ramu, but they are of about the same age. Her expression is mild and absorbed, and she often wears a thin smile across her face. The husband and wife have no children and have no desire either.

How and why Ramu and Sughandha married is a completely different story. In truth, Ramu had no choice in marrying Sughandha, but only the couple know the full details. It was an unusual set of circumstances for which there was never a clear answer. Once again, if you ask Ramu, you will always get a different response. "I lost a bet." "I drank too much one night and woke up with a ring on my finger." "I did it to save the whales. Pollution kills, you know!"

Anika walks down the crowded corridor holding the picture in front of herself. She tries squinting as if this would make the black and white photo clearer. Then, by the side of the track, Anika sees an elderly man. He is wearing the very same baseball cap as the young man in the photo. Anika can't believe herself. She gives a quick laugh and almost jumps up with both feet. The young lady is swift in her movements, and she does not hesitate. Anika approaches the elderly man and notices that he has no hair or teeth. He is sitting on his tattered suitcase, looking down into his old, withered hands.

"Uncle? Is your name Raj?" she asks.

"No, I am Dev Anand," the old man looks up and replies with a toothless smile.

Anika frowns and steps back. She feels hopeless. Her excitement begins to fade as she realizes how pointless her mission is. There is no way to find an individual you have never met in a crowded station with nothing but an old photo. Discouraged, she sits down, crossed-legged in the middle of the station, facing the stairs to the exit. To her left is the northbound track. To her right is the southbound track. She scans left and right with her gaze and then thinks to herself, "If Uncle Raj wants to get back home, he come and find me."

After a while, the crowd starts to dissipate. Anika then sees a man sitting, legs crossed on the station floor. To his left is the northbound track. To his right is the southbound track. And he is also facing the exit, so the man's back is towards Anika. The young lady stands up and begins to approach this gentleman from behind. She comes around to meet him, and then she frowns. This man doesn't match her father's description of Raj either. Also, he looks much younger than her father.

The man has a pure countenance and a calm demeanour. He is wearing a maroon t-shirt, with black denim jeans. He has a full head of hair, and modern, yet simple spectacles rest upon his face. He wears light blue **sneakers**, clean but worn with age. There is also a small hole at the top of the left shoe, near the big toe. He does not have any luggage except for a medium-sized backpack. Puzzled, Anika turns and begins to walk away.

The man then shouts out "Anika!" as the young lady heads up the stairs.

With hesitation, she turns and then pauses for a moment. "Uncle Raj?" she yells back. At first, Anika regrets saying anything. The young lady thinks that she must have misunderstood the man, and she begins to feel foolish. The train station is still loud even though it is less crowded now. And the horn of the next arriving train makes it difficult to hear. The man is now standing, and he bends over to pick up his backpack. "It can't be Raj," the young lady tells herself. Anika shakes her head and turns back towards the remaining steps ahead.

"Where's Prakash?" he then calls out.

She hears him this time. Anika jumps down the steps and lands in front of Raj with a big smile on her face. She is relieved more than anything, and it shows. "At home," Anika says. "He can't wait to see you! How did you know it was me?"

"Facebook. What else?" Raj smiles back.

Raj refuses help from the luggage handler on the platform, and they head towards the pickup area.

The Ice Cream

Anika points out the automobile that is stuck in traffic towards the exit of the station. Raj opens the trunk and throws his backpack inside. He then opens the door for Anika, closes the door behind her, and walks up to the driver's open window.

Raj sticks out his hand to the driver. "Hi, I'm Raj. Pleased to meet you."

Ramu responds, imitating Amitabh Bachchan. Raj gives a hearty laugh, walks around the front, and takes the seat next to the driver.

Once they are all in the car, Ramu delivers a story, again impersonating Amitabh Bachchan. He tells Raj how he came to be the family's personal bodyguard, starting at Anika's grandfather's farm as a caretaker. At some point, Anika must stop Ramu's diatribe, and Ramu finally starts to drive home.

On their way home, Raj mentions how he knew Anika's dad. "Your father was very studious, you know," Raj began. "Even if we were partying all night, he would be the first one up to study."

This perks Anika's interest, and she leans forward, "Wait, Daddy used to party all night? Tell me more."

Raj realizes that he is on thin ice, so he backtracks. He clears his throat as if his mouth is dry. Then after a pause, he finally continues, "What I mean is that even if Prakash were up all night, helping friends to move, or watching late-night movies, or whatever, he would still rise early the next day to hit the books."

Anika gives a hearty laugh, "Right, helping friends move late at night. Makes total sense, Uncle."

Raj turns a bit red, and changes the topic, "So young lady, what are you up to these days?"

Anika cannot help herself, "Oh, nothing much. Mostly just watch late night movies." She laughs again, but then she lets Raj off the hook. "But really, I'm just trying to figure out what I want to do next with myself."

"The good news is that you have your whole life to figure that out. I'm older than your father, and I'm still trying to figure my life out. Life is not a race, right?"

"Right." Anika shrugs, as if unsure of herself. She had never heard an adult say that to her before, so it gives her pause. The young lady rests back in her seat and takes a deep breath and lets out a long sigh. She then leans forward again. She puts her hand on Raj's left shoulder, "Raj, let's bring home some ice cream before we head back."

Raj smiles and faces back, and he cheers, "Sounds like a plan." He gives her the thumbs up.

The Pretty Hair

Upon Anika and Raj's arrival, they find the whole family waiting for their guest.

Ramu (this time impersonating a government official) gives the introductions. "This is Ramla, the best chef in town. And this is his wife, Mangla. She can vacuum the rugs and fold clothes at the same time. Blindfolded. They have been together for over thirty years. And this is my wife, Sughandha. She's practicing to become a stay-at-home librarian." As usual, Ramu's wife does not feign interest. She keeps on reading her book after looking up for a split second and giving a quick smile to Raj.

Ramu escorts the guest into the living room. But before moving on, Raj moves up to Ramla first and shakes his hand. "Pleased to meet you, Ramla! I haven't had a good meal in over a thousand kilometres. I hope you can change that." Raj hands Ramu the ice cream. Raj then takes both of Mangla's hands in his, "Mangla, I have never seen such pretty hair. You must tell me the name of your stylist. I'm well overdue."

Mangla beams and smiles back at her husband with an affirming nod. As the guest turns and walks towards the living room, the maid elbows her husband as if to say, "Did you hear what he said about me?" Although she does not say anything out loud, her expression is clear. It has been a long time since someone complimented her, and Mangla makes it clear that one was well overdue. Ramla gives a small frown, and a gruff as he turns to head towards the kitchen with the ice cream.

Now, Ramu escorts Raj into the living room, with Anika following them both.

"And here's Meena! It's been a long time since you've seen each other, right?"

"Meena! Thank you for inviting me to your home." Raj gives a courteous bow.

"It's been too long, Raj. I was afraid you had disappeared." **Meena** is unable to move. Her feet feel heavy under her body. And her heart swells with elation, but also sorrow.

"I know," Raj avows.

Prakash walks in from his office.

"And here's..." Ramu continues.

Without Ramu having to finish, Raj and Prakash embrace each other. They then tap each other's back with a fist and look at each other with misty eyes.

"Welcome, my friend! It's been half a lifetime. Too long! My, you have not changed one bit," Prakash exclaims.

Raj jokes and rubs his friend's belly as if for good luck. "I can't say the same for you, Prakash. But you have the same smile, so I know it's you." Raj then turns to Meena, "You look younger than when I last saw you. You must tell me your secret. I also see you've been taking good care of my friend."

Meena smirks and chortles, "Well, if I don't feed him enough, he'll be up all night looking for food."

Ramu entertains them by mimicking Sanjeev Kumar. They have some ice cream. And the two friends feed each other. Anika bubbles with excitement, as she enjoys Raj's jovial humour and carefree attitude.

The Present

After brunch, the guest decides to get some rest. Anika and Ramu lead Raj to his accommodations in the pool house. It is a good-sized structure with a private entrance and bathroom. It is opposite the garden and faces the back of the main house. Inside, it is contemporary and modern. The interior resembles a hotel room designed by Ikea. The furniture is minimal and functional, but stylish and sleek.

There is a king-sized bed, topped with a light-green blanket on the far end. And next to the bed is the bathroom door. And there are two armchairs, also with light-green upholstery and a side table near the entrance. On the side table, there's a chessboard with the pieces paused in mid-play. Between the armchairs and the bed, there is a bookcase. It is full of books except for the top row, where a single plant, a white orchid, sits on top.

"This is my favourite room in the house," Anika admits. She walks over to the bookcases. "When I want to get away, I come in here and pick up a book and just get lost in it."

"Okay, Anika. Take it from here. I'm going to get the cars washed." Ramu turns towards Raj, "It is a pleasure to meet you, Raj." For some reason, he gives Raj a military-style salute.

The guest stands at attention, and returns the salute, "The pleasure has been mine, sir." And Ramu makes his exit.

Just For You

Given the long overnight train ride, exhaustion begins to weigh heavy on Raj. He can feel his feet become cumbersome underneath his body as he struggles to move towards the bed. He welcomes the opportunity to get some much-needed rest. Raj glances at the shelves of books, but he cannot concentrate enough to even read any of the titles.

Raj places his bag on the armchair that is closer to the bed. He struggles to smile as he faces Anika, still near the bookcase. "Thank you both. I'll rest now, so I'm all fresh and ready to party this evening."

Anika feels elated to have Raj as their new guest. It has been a long time since the young lady had someone visit the home who treats her like an equal and like an adult. And most importantly, like a friend.

As Anika leaves the guest house, she pauses and asks him a question. "Uncle Raj, since this is the first time you're meeting me, did you bring me a present?"

"No, I didn't," Raj falters as he steps towards the bed. His eyes begin to close on their own, and he struggles to keep them open. "I'm sorry. I had no idea what to bring. But one day, I will be more than happy to buy you a gift of your choice."

Raj then reaches into his backpack. He pulls out a cone-shaped packet of roasted peanuts and beans from the train station and hands it to Anika. "Just for you."

Anika accepts the gift with a gracious smile. "Oh, thank you!" She steps back with a bounce. "Be sure to be ready by five p.m., Uncle. Do you have a formal suit and tie?"

"In Goa," Raj replies, "there are only two occasions when individuals wear a suit and tie." He now sits on the bed and begins to take off his shoes and socks. "Church weddings and funerals." After a pause, he continues, "I know we're not having a funeral tonight, so tell me, Anika, is today your wedding? And where's the church?"

Anika, unable to control her smile, shakes her head no. She blushes a bit.

"Well, not to worry." The man now lies on his back on the bed and puts his feet up. "I'll just have to wear something comfortable." Once he finishes laying down, Raj remembers something important. "I do have one request, dear."

"Yes, Uncle?" Anika perks up and leans forward, her hand on the back of the light-green armchair near the exit.

"Kindly tell Ramu to bring me masala tea at four p.m."

"You got it, Raj Uncle!" And the young lady walks out the door. Before Anika has the door to the entrance closed behind herself, Raj falls fast asleep.

The Preparation

Meanwhile, in the main house, Prakash and Meena are frantic. They are busy zooming left and right, finalizing the preparations for the party.

The matriarch oversees the appetizer stands, which Ramla, the family's head chef, will prepare with his staff. There will be three distinct stations serving various Indian dishes. The first station will serve *chana chaat*. The appetizer is famous all over the subcontinent, so Meena thinks it will be a safe bet. The hors d'oeuvre is a refreshing and tangy combination of chickpeas (*chana*), potatoes, tomatoes, and onions.

The second station will serve finger food spread across a large circular tray. *Samosas*, a crispy pastry turnover filled with spiced vegetables, will form the perimeter. The middle ring will contain various *pakoras*. These are onion fritters combined with either cauliflower, spinach, or *paneer* (fresh cheese). Prakash considers alternatives to the *pakoras*, but the wife pushes back. The fritters are a must-have in her mind. And finally, *papadam* will rest in the centre of the tray. This is a thin and crispy lentil flatbread with a bit of garlic and a bit of spice. To prepare, the *papadam* rests over a hot stove for two minutes until it becomes piping hot and crunchy.

Finally, the third station will serve *dosa*, made to order, so that it is hot and fresh. It resembles a big, thin crepe, but it is filled with spiced potatoes. To prepare, Ramla will spread the batter on a large pan. It will become super thin and crispy when heated. But the *dosa* will taste like sourdough bread because of the fermented rice and lentils that make up the batter. This last station is sure to delight, Meena thinks to herself.

The wife then coordinates the timing of the meals with Ramla. Finally, she ensures that the silverware is clean and ready.

Meanwhile, the patriarch selects the music arrangements. Prakash plans the evening's music as if he is composing an opera. Prakash directs Ramu, who will serve as the evening's opera conductor (DJ).

"I want the first hour to be mellow and calm," he picks out a few compact discs from his massive collection. "Here, begin with these." He hands Ramu a few instrumental tracks. "Make sure to blend the songs according to proper mood and tempo."

"You got it, sir! I'll consider it an honour," Ramu salutes Prakash.

Prakash does not notice Ramu's antics. He is oblivious that Ramu is now making faces behind his back. Prakash continues, "But once all the guests arrive, I want something with energy. Something lively." He hands Ramu another stack of compact disks. "Here. Sort through these and pick out the latest *Bollywood* hits from twenty-five years ago."

"Finally, to wind down the evening, I want something mellow," the husband continues.

He picks out another giant stack of compact discs. From this stack, Prakash hands Ramu a selection of classical pieces from Ravi Shankar. These sentimental works feature long *ragas* filled with evolving beats and improvised melodies. Prakash often plays *ragas* on Saturday mornings, after a long week of work to unwind and zone out. But to close out the evening, he thinks that this will set the right mood. Something classy, yet ambient.

Ramu has a puzzled look on his face, "I guess I have some homework to do before the party. I'll get on top of it, sir."

Prakash slaps his back, "That a boy. Don't think of it as homework. Think of it more as an adventure."

As the husband turns to leave, Ramu crosses his eyes and sticks his tongue out. Once again, the patriarch is oblivious to Ramu's antics.

Prakash then turns his attention to the bar. He ensures that it is well stocked. Finally, the husband prepares an area near the dining table for the toast, which will take place after dinner.

Anika enters and adds her own colour and flair to everything she encounters. "Mommy, would you like to place the cake near the stage? Daddy, please keep the music to this century. You both need to get dressed soon. Go upstairs and get ready. I'll finish down here."

"You know," the daughter says to her father, "Uncle Raj doesn't have a suit. He came with only a backpack."

Prakash laughs. "Yeah, I know Raj. That's just like him. Take him my newly tailored suit from the front closet. The grey one with two buttons."

The Movie Star

After a long nap, Raj awakens in an unfamiliar bed. At first, his body feels heavy, as if he is wearing a lead vest and about to get his teeth X-rayed by a dentist. But the room is bright. Daylight streams in through the window next to the door near the entrance. The guest is hazy as if he has been sleeping for a long time, but soon, the fog begins to lift, and after a minute, he manages to sit up. "That's right. It's party time," Raj reminds himself.

These days, Raj is not a fan of big parties, but he is glad for the opportunity to catch up with his once close friend. Raj then heads towards the bathroom to get ready. He takes a shower. And he washes his hair. He then places a facial mask on his face and waits for Ramu to bring him his four p.m. tea.

The bell rings, and Raj opens the pool house door. Anika enters with the grey suit and the tea. Raj looks embarrassed to see the young lady. He is in a bathrobe with a white facial mask covering his face. And running into Raj in this state gives Anika an incredible laugh.

"Uncle Raj, you really are a movie star," she chortles, placing the suit on the bed. The young lady then places the tea on the side table with the chessboard on it.

Raj's face turns red. But the white facial mask hides his embarrassment. Yet, he turns and runs to the bathroom with a quiet shriek. Anika walks back to the main house smiling, but she decides to keep the hilarity to herself.

The Dress

It is now five p.m., and the guests have started to arrive. The family is ready at the entrance to welcome them. Even the cook, Ramla, and his wife (the maid), Mangla, are in a festive mood.

Ramu is the party's foremost entertainment. As the guests begin to fill the atrium, he keeps them entertained with his impersonations. And every now and then, Ramu changes the music playing on the sound system.

Prakash and Meena continue to invite guests in from the entrance of the house. Anika is busy sampling the hors d'oeuvres. But the young lady is also awaiting Uncle Raj's arrival as she is curious to see what he will be wearing.

Raj makes a timely entrance, and he wears a gentle smile across his face. He feels rested and energetic. Raj then proceeds to chat with Ramu. And then he greets Ramla and Mangla. "Great masala tea, Ramla! The best!"

Ramla smiles with appreciation, and he winks at Mangla as if to say, "I too can get a compliment now and then."

At the bar, Raj eyes Anika. She is wearing a simple but beautiful and elegant *Anarkali* dress. The dress is all black with netted sleeves and an orange border. For a moment, Raj becomes entranced, unable to take his eyes off her.

Anika sees Raj, and she rushes to welcome him. For a moment, they pause and stare at each other in the eyes. Raj wants to tell her that she looks beautiful, but he whispers it in his mind instead.

The young lady is happy. And for some reason, she is also relieved. Anika is delighted to see that Raj is wearing a sharp, well-fitting outfit. He is wearing black designer jeans, a black shirt, and a classic-blue sports coat. Polished leather shoes with rusty metal straps for shoes. And a rustic leather belt, with a large rusty metal belt buckle, completes his attire.

Anika looks him up and down as he walks towards her. "You clean up well, Uncle Raj. Very dapper! Where did you get the sports coat?"

Raj smiles. "Thank you." He pauses for a moment, "It's surprising what you can fit inside a backpack if you fold it well."

"Follow me," she takes his hand. After greeting each other, the young lady proceeds to take Raj by her side, and she guides him to the different food stalls.

The Eggs

Party guests include friends and family of Prakash and Meena. Also, many of Prakash's hospital colleagues and office staff attended the celebration. The doctor's secretary, Vijaya Laxmi, makes a blaring entrance. She is tall, big, and round. Her hair is curly and messy, like a self-inflicted perm. And she always wears colourful, gaudy outfits.

Today, the secretary is wearing a bright pink dress and a purple shawl. Neither match, but this does not bother Vijaya. She is full of excitement, and she cannot help but greet everyone the moment they enter. It is as if the party was her own, and she was the only host.

The guests mingle and begin to settle in. Libations disperse, and the aroma of tasty food fills the air. Vijaya makes her way towards the first stall, and yells across the room, "Meena, any eggs in the *chana chaat*?"

"No, Vijaya Laxmi," Meena answers. "The *chaat* does not have any eggs in it."

"Meena, any chicken in the *samosas*?" she hollers back.

"No, Vijaya Laxmi. The *samosas* are not made with chicken."

This continues a few more times.

Meena then walks over and introduces Raj to Vijaya. "Vijaya, I would like you to meet Raj. He's visiting from Goa."

Before Raj can respond, Vijaya asks, "Raj, any meat in these *pakoras*?"

"No," Raj responds, "these are all vegetarian dishes, Vijaya."

"Raj, any eggs in the *paneer*?"

"No, this is a vegetarian dish, Vijaya."

This continues a few more times.

Anika notices Raj's impending frustration. She pulls him aside and whispers into his ear, "The only way to get Vijaya to stop is to tell her yes."

A few minutes later, Vijaya bumps into Raj once again. This time she is enjoying her *dosa*. Unable to help herself, she asks, "Raj, any eggs in the *dosa*?"

"No," Raj responds, "this is a vegetarian dish, Vijaya." After a pause, he continues, "Your dosa was made with only vegetarian eggs."

Vijaya's face turns white. Fear and disbelief are visible across her expressive face. She gasps, "But you just said this is a vegetarian dish."

"It is, Vijaya," Raj replies. "The eggs came from one hundred percent vegan chickens. The hens grew up on a non-GMO, vegetarian diet."

Vijaya becomes angry and scared at the same time. "But that's not the same thing!" She panics and runs to the corner of the living room to pray.

The Swami

The party picks up, and most of the guests now have arrived. Prakash forgets about his commands to Ramu about the music, as expected. So, Ramu plays his own playlist. The music is instrumental but mixed with modern beats. It provides a warm ambiance and a casual atmosphere. And the guests enjoy the drifting conversation. The yummy food fills their bellies, and the bottomless drinks lift their spirits. The evening begins to liven.

Ramu entertains the office staff. In another life, he would be practicing stand-up comedy. He loves the opportunity to make others laugh and unwind. And a party such as this one gives him a perfect chance to try out his new material.

The comedian's jokes are conventional, by most standards, but his execution is perfect. Ramu has this uncanny ability to not laugh at his own antics, which only adds to his gravitas. A true performer, he can read the crowd like a thermometer, and he can breathe life into any situation. Anika often jokes, "I want Ramu to give my eulogy when I pass away."

Sughandha, Ramu's wife, never laughs at her husband's jokes. She considers them lame and trite. At present, she is sitting in a corner with her book, oblivious to her surroundings as usual. The visible recluse is about two-thirds of the way through *Madame Bovary* by Gustave Flaubert.

Sugandha feels a connection with the novel's main character, who is also of two minds. The Madame longs for unadulterated freedom. To be like a soaring eagle. One that climbs above the clouds at will. And then flies off into the endless blue sky. Sughandha too wants to escape her destiny. But also like the Madame, she wants to revel in solitude, and borrow deep down, like a mole that is allergic to fresh air. Sughandha gives a tiny sigh. And she turns the page with comforting remorse in her mind and sorrow in her heart. And she continues reading.

Prakash and Meena are mingling in opposite corners of the room, chatting with the guests. Anika wants to pick up a conversation with Raj, but she has no idea where to begin. Raj is leaning against the side of the couch, but not talking with anyone in particular. He has a peaceful countenance as if he were surveying the view from on top of a mountain. And his brow is relaxed, and he is smiling to himself.

Finally, Anika walks up to Raj and taps him on his shoulder. He turns around to face the young lady.

"Thank you, Raj, for your gift. The roasted peanuts and beans were yummy."

Raj's face turns a bit red. Raj is overcome with embarrassment. And he quavers with care in his voice but a lump forms in his throat, "I wish I had brought you more, Anika. Next time, I'll bring you a stylish handbag."

"No need, Raj. It's the thought that matters to me the most. I really do appreciate it."

The two pause, still facing each other. Raj is speechless but wants to continue the conversation. Of course, they both knew that the packet of roasted snack was not meant for the young lady. Raj cannot overcome his guilt, but at the same time, he realizes how silly it is to feel guilty about such a thing. Yet, Raj takes note of Anika's genuine sincerity. And this embarrasses Raj even more.

Anika notices some dye remaining on Raj's forehead. "He must have overlooked it when he dyed his hair earlier that day," she thinks to herself.

Without hesitation, Anika takes a napkin, dips it in her cup. She then proceeds to wipe the smudge away from Raj's upper brow.

Raj's embarrassment climbs even higher, and at this point, the young lady is leaning in very close to him. Raj can smell her fragrance, feel her warmth, and sense her beauty, but he does not dare to say anything.

Raj's face is now clean. Anika then tugs his hand and takes him to a small line in front of the *dosa* stall. "I hope you don't mind all of the vegetarian food, Uncle Raj?"

"Why should I mind? I'm a vegetarian, after all."

Anika is curious. "Oh, may I ask why?"

"I used to eat a lot of meat, chicken, and seafood," Raj explains, "until one day a Swami asked me if I ate meat."

Anika, even more curious, responds, "What did you say, Uncle?"

"I told the Swami, 'Of course I eat meat. Meat's natural; it comes from nature.' "

"And how did the Swami respond?"

"The Swami told me, 'It is not right to take a life if you cannot give one.' This stuck with me, and since that day, I haven't touched meat."

"Wow! Really?" Anika feels mesmerized at this notion.

"Yes, not even eggs."

Anika and Raj happen to look in the direction of Vijaya Laxmi at this moment, who is still in the corner, praying.

"Even if the eggs are vegetarian?" chuckled the young lady, staring across the room.

The two look back and into each other's eyes. They both smile and give a small laugh at the same time.

The Serving Dish

Everyone is having a great time. And now it is time for the cake cutting ceremony. The guests gather in the dining room, where three cakes sit on top of a medium-sized side table with a white tablecloth on top.

Ramu, in the magnanimous voice of Ashok Kumar, begins. "Welcome, friends, family, colleagues, and distant travellers. I wish to welcome you to the distinguished home of our hosts, Prakash and Meena."

By chance, Raj and Anika are standing opposite each other, and both are smiling at each other.

Prakash takes over. "Thank you, Ramu. And thank you, everyone, for coming over this evening to celebrate with us. Also, I want to thank my close family for all of the efforts you put into tonight in helping to make it a success."

The guests clap.

Prakash continues, "This is an incredible day to me for three reasons. First, it's my fiftieth birthday."

The guests clap again, and a few guests cheer.

"Second, it's our twenty-fifth anniversary."

The guests clap again, and this time, a few of them whistle.

"Third, and most importantly, after twenty-five years, I have reconnected with my long-lost friend, Raj."

Sensing importance, the guests cheer with volume.

"Raj and I lived in the same dorm on campus, even though Raj was not a medical student. This man had an insatiable curiosity for all subjects and attended almost every class offered by the university."

The host turns towards Raj and gives him a wink. "But I'm not sure how many he actually passed," Prakash belts out with a smirk.

The guests give a hearty laugh to this.

And Prakash now looks out across the crowd, and then his eyes lock with Meena's. The husband becomes emotional and continues in a low voice. "And if it were not for Raj, I would not be here today."

The guests, boisterous moments ago, now become quiet and solemn.

Prakash recounts, "One summer during my first year in medical school, we were having a college-wide picnic on Madh Island, just outside the city. It was evening, and the sun was going down, but boy, were we having a good time."

Prakash looks in Raj's direction, and the friend nods back, with emotion in his eyes. Raj recalled that fateful day very recently, on the train ride into town. Raj recalled the distinct taste of salt swell up into his lungs and deep into his stomach. Raj had that same feeling at this very moment. For some unknown reason, he also feels queasy and uneasy.

Prakash proceeds, "I almost drowned that day. A storm came in out of nowhere, and the sea almost ate me for dinner."

Meena knew this story well, but Anika had no idea. The daughter feels a sudden mix of strong emotions, but most of all, she feels fear. She had never contemplated her father's mortality. And thinking about it in this way makes her heart sink. Tears begin to swell in her eyes, and she turns to wipe them away.

Prakash looks back across the crowd, "If it were not for Raj, I would be at the bottom of the ocean right now. I owe him more than you can imagine. And I can only hope to be able to repay him one day for all that he has done for me." The host then puts his arm around his wife and pulls her towards his side and pulls her shoulder towards his. Meena is also emotional at this point.

The host holds up his glass. "To my wife, my daughter, my gracious guests, and to you, Raj. Cheers!"

The guests, in unison, exclaim, "Cheers!"

The patriarch, with moist eyes, waves Raj to come forward. Raj steps up and stands next to Prakash.

"Hi, I'm Raj. Pleased to meet you all. I hope I never find myself in such a situation as Prakash found himself that day long ago. But I also know in my heart that Prakash would have done the same for me if the tables were turned. Thank you, Prakash. You are a true friend."

The crowd applauses with reverence.

Prakash and Raj embrace. And then they cut the three cakes. One for Prakash, one for Meena, and one for Raj.

Soon after, Vijaya Laxmi comes up to Raj and asks, "Raj, any eggs in the cake?"

Raj replies, "Not only eggs but also chicken. But don't worry, both are organic."

Vijaya Laxmi cries, "Oh no!" A piece of cake falls from the woman's mouth, mid-bite. She runs back to the corner and begins her prayers all over again.

In the meantime, the family members, Raj included, feed each other cake.

As the guests are finishing the cake, Ramu calls out, "Guests, please gather around. I would like to sing a special song for our anniversary couple."

Ramu sits Prakash and Meera down on chairs facing each other. The lights dim, and Ramu begins to sing *Aye Meri Zohra Jabeen* from the movie *Waqt*.

The husband and wife stand and begin to dance. The guests join in the dancing. Just then, a large serving dish falls from the top of the bookcase at the end of the hallway, creating a loud bang.

Ramu stops singing midway through a line. On one side of the bookcase is Sughandha, uninterrupted and engrossed in her book. On the other is Raj and Anika, engrossed in a lively debate.

For a moment, all eyes are on the couple. And both of their faces turn bright red. But in the next moment, Ramu resumes singing as if nothing happened as Raj and Anika begin to clean up the mess.

It is now late, almost midnight. Many of the guests with children at home have already left. Most of the others begin to trickle out the door.

Meena has not stopped to rest all night, and so the fatigue begins to catch up with her. In fact, she is the only one who has not eaten yet, except for a few nibbles of food here and there. She has an exhausted look across her face, yet she is glad that the party went off without a hitch.

During a conversation with Sunil Dhawan, Meena learned of a job opening at his practice. Sunil is a former colleague of Prakash who now runs a medical clinic that is close by. "It would be perfect if Anika could gain some experience there," Meena thinks to herself. She plans to tell her daughter about it first thing.

But the mother knows her daughter well. If Meena were to sound too excited about the opportunity, Anika would dismiss it. So the mother begins to calculate a plan to bring up the position. "Tomorrow, over tea, will be perfect. I'll sneak it in after she's nice and rested," Meena thinks to herself. At the same time, she begins to pick up the silverware and plates from around the house. She transports them to the kitchen and instructs the staff to start clearing the food away.

The party winds down and the general mood becomes less animated and more drowsy. But bellies are full and spirits are tipsy. The remaining guests feel satiated and tired from the night's events. They too begin to leave. Raj makes his way towards the exit of the house, where he meets Meena and Anika, and calls out, "Goodnight, ladies!"

They nod back but are too drained to respond with words.

Yet Raj still asks a question, "Meena, by the way, is there a jogging track nearby?"

As Meena is about to respond, Anika interrupts. "Well, there is, but not for you," she smirks.

"And why not?" Raj inquires.

"It's very hilly," Anika replies. "Way too steep for a novice."

"That's exactly what I like."

Anika holds out her hand. "Great, we'll head out at seven a.m."

Before even Raj or Meena can process the situation, the young lady shakes Raj's hand. He then nods to Anika and Meena and walks out the backdoor, towards the pool house.

The Seagull

Around seven a.m. the next day, both Raj and Anika are ready for their morning run. The day is bright, but the sun is not yet intense. The air is thick and humid. So thick that you can almost cut it with a knife. Or scoop it up with a spoon. Even so, it is a pleasant day for a jog across the hills of New Mumbai.

Raj meets Anika in front of the main house. The young lady is wearing a sporty neon-green top with white tennis shorts. Raj is wearing track pants and an old T-shirt with Carpe Diem written in big letters across the top.

The guest is already sweating from the heat. Raj's mind feels energized, but his body is still waking up. Yet he looks forward to some healthy exercise after last night's festivities. Anika is in a bright and peppery mood. She hands Raj a bottle of water. "Just for you. In case you start to feel faint."

They both laugh and head towards the jogging trail. The trail begins at the top of a steep embankment. It is a winding dirt path, where vegetation hangs from all sides. But every now and then you can see the ocean through the dense foliage. And the sound of the bustling city is always close by.

Merchants make their way across the path as they too begin the day. And school children, in groups of five or six, carry stacks of books in their arms. But the trail is not an easy one. An amateur would find it to be quite challenging.

But to Anika's surprise, Raj turns out to be a solid runner. The pair makes their way up and down the cliffside, and they both take notice of the seagulls near the top of the trail. It is here that they sit to rest and pause for a few moments to take in the day before turning around again.

"With a view like this, it almost makes the journey up here worth it," Raj smirks, out of breath.

"This city is filled with hidden jewels like this one," Anika reflects with a bit of sorrow and sentiment.

As they look out over the embankment, the young lady spots a lonely seagull trying its best to catch up with the flock. The bird darts forward, but it cannot keep up with the others. And so it breaks away and shoots down towards the shimmering water below. And so the gull takes a rest on a passing sailboat, where it finds a new resting place away from the others.

The Gift

After the run, Raj and Anika return to the house, dripping with sweat. As they enter the home, they see that everyone is up. And the rest of the family is enjoying breakfast around the coffee table in the living room.

Prakash is reading the Sunday paper, and Meena is sorting through the gifts. Everyone is in a relaxed mood, and the family begins to open the presents from last night's event.

Prakash places a gift box shaped like a cube in front of himself. And he sets a similar-sized gift in front of Meena. Prakash gestures to Raj and Anika. "Here, grab those and open them up."

The daughter takes a rectangular shaped gift box from the pile and hands it to Raj. She places another similar sized one in front of herself. At about the same time, Prakash, Meena, Anika, and Raj unwrap and open their respective presents.

The husband and wife each find similar fancy candles in their gift boxes. The daughter and Raj each take notice of the same picture frame in each of their boxes. The four look at each other and shrug their shoulders. They all share a common understanding when it comes to the unoriginality of boxed gifts.

The mother then grabs another present from the pile. This one turns out to be a vase. In fact, it is the same vase that is filled with flowers in the centre of the coffee table.

Meena turns to her husband. "Didn't we give this same vase to the Shahs last year, Prakash?" She then turns the lid to the box in front of her over. Meena then notices a tag under the ribbon. "See, it even says here, 'From Prakash and Meena.'"

Anika observes, "Funny, the Shahs weren't even here last night. They're still vacationing in Nepal."

Prakash responds while smiling, "That's always the case with boxed gifts. What goes around, comes around."

"Well, Daddy, what did you get for Mommy to celebrate your anniversary?" the daughter asks.

Prakash looks stumped, having forgotten to get anything.

The wife knows her husband too well, and she lets him off the hook. Meena places her left hand on her husband's side, and her right hand on her daughter's head. "Anika, I already have everything in life. You are my greatest gift."

With some emotion, Anika gives Meena a hug. "Mommy, you are more than a mother to me. You are my true friend."

At last, they get to the final gift. It is the biggest box. Anika opens the bulky item. Inside is a large pile of colourful packing paper. And at its centre is a small envelope, which she hands to Prakash.

Prakash opens the envelope and reads the card inside of it. "Dear Prakash, thanks for taking such great care of my patients. Sincerely, Dr. Bhatia."

Anika points to the back of the card. "Daddy, it looks like there's something on the back of the card."

Prakash turns the card over. "You're right. It's a gift card for the Maharaja Grill."

"Awesome," Anika exclaims, "isn't that like an eight-star restaurant?"

"It is," Meena muses. "How generous, Prakash!"

The father agrees, "Yes, I must thank him at work tomorrow."

Excitement permeates the room. Anika tells her father, "Amazing! You should take Mommy for a nice dinner."

"Yes," The husband shrugs, "I guess I'll check my schedule, and we'll choose a date."

At this point, Raj goes back to the guest house and comes back with his anniversary gifts for the couple. He hands one small box to the husband and the other small box to the wife.

They open their boxes at the same time. "Wow, Rolex!" they exclaim.

Prakash, Meena, and Anika are all surprised. "Raj," Meena says, "this is too much. We cannot possibly accept such lavish gifts."

"Thank you, Raj," Prakash says. "I don't know what to say. How did you manage to get hold of such beautiful items?"

"As you know, I run a small hotel in Goa," Raj notes. "Well, from time to time, we get tourists from overseas who pawn expensive items after losing money in the floating casino next to my hotel. Happens more often than you would think."

"But Raj, these still have the tags on them," Meena observes, perplexed.

"Sometimes, you just get lucky," Raj suggests.

Taken aback, the patriarch hands the restaurant gift card to Raj. "Here, take this and go have a good night out." He then turns to his daughter. "Anika, I want you to take Raj to the Maharaja Grill for a nice dinner."

"That's very kind of you, Prakash," Raj says. "But why don't all four of us go?"

"I'm on call tonight," the father replies, "but that's no reason why you should be stuck at home."

"No rush," Raj responds. "We can go another night."

"I insist, Raj," he declares. "You and Anika have a good time. Anika, make sure our guest enjoys himself."

"Okay, Daddy. Uncle Raj, have you ever been around Mumbai at night?"

Raj turns to Anika. "No, I'm a small city guy."

The excitement fills Anika's head. "Well then, you're in for a good time. You'll love it. Remember to wear something fancy. The Grill is beyond extravagant."

"Will do."

"It's settled then," Prakash says, turning to Ramu. "Ramu, you'll drop them off."

"Yes, sir." Ramu salutes.

The Fragrance

In the evening, Raj walks towards the front of the house, where he meets Anika, who is ready to go. She is leaning on the car and taking in the refreshing mist from the bustling fountain in front of her.

Raj wears a navy-blue button-down, collared shirt with black pants. The shirt seems to sparkle like the stars above. And his hair is wet but tidy, and his shoes are clean and shiny. Anika is wearing a simple but elegant black dress, with matching black heels with velvet straps. And her hair is in a bun, and on her long neck is a simple pendant that also sparkles in the moonlight.

Ramu is checking the car's fluids under the hood. Sughandha is already in the front passenger seat. She is reading a novel, of course. This time, she finds herself deep within the world of Hogwarts. She has read the Harry Potter series countless times. So at this point, she looks at a page and knows what is going on without having to read the actual words. Even so, she does not dare to look beyond the pages of the book on her lap.

The guest walks up to the young lady, who looks him up and down. "Sharp, Uncle Raj!"

"Thank you." Raj thinks about giving her a compliment but decides against it.

Raj opens the car door and allows Anika to enter the back seat. He closes the door and walks around the back of the car to get in from the other side. As he is walking around, Anika leans over to unlock his door. Raj opens his door and takes a seat in the back.

Ramu then closes the hood. He is surprised to see everyone already in the car, ready to go. And so he gives an approving nod. The driver then impersonates a cowboy and says, "Giddy up guys and gals!"

The chauffeur steps in the car, and they set off. While in the car, Raj turns to Anika. "You smell nice."

"Just for you, Uncle," she gives a thin smile.

"Do you like my cologne?" Raj asks. "It's trendy in Goa these days."

She leans in to take a sniff.

Anika responds in a not-too-impressed voice. "Oh, what cologne is that?"

"Mosquito repellent," Raj smirks. "It's nice and fragrant, plus it prevents mosquito bites. Two benefits for the price of one."

"I see. That's very sensible and economical of you," the young lady chuckles.

"Plus, I hear that mosquitoes love hanging out at eight-star restaurants."

Ramu laughs out loud at this. But then he gives a small grunt and turns his attention away. He knows well that he should not be eavesdropping on the conversations of his passengers.

Even so, Raj and Anika notice Ramu turn away, and they both laugh as well. Sughandha is oblivious, as usual. But the mood is light, and the party continues onwards to the restaurant.

The Coy

The car pulls up to the entrance of the Maharaja Grill. The restaurant has a long driveway, lined with palm trees and flowers. And the sound of running water permeates the building's facade. It is a commanding structure, with intricate carvings reminiscent of an ancient palace. At the entrance to the restaurant is a big wooden door, three times the size one would ever need.

The doorman, dressed in black pants, a white shirt, with a red vest and red bow-tie, comes to open the door for Raj. As the doorman opens Raj's door, Raj says to him, "Ladies first!"

The doorman nods and shuts Raj's door. He then goes around to the other side of the car and opens the door for Anika. Anika steps out of the vehicle. Ramu starts driving off with Raj still in the backseat.

He grunts to alert Ramu of his presence. Ramu responds, impersonating Om Prakash this time. "You're in trouble now, Raj. You have no choice but to walk back up the hill to the restaurant."

Back at the restaurant entrance, the young lady waits for Raj. And as she waits, she takes in the lush surroundings, and she also takes notice of the stream of flowing water under her feet. Wooden planks that support her legs connect the valet station to the entrance. And a pond with colourful coy fills the basin below. The fish seem to be at peace as they meander and dart back and forth. They move with intent but without care at the same time.

Anika often feels anxious and inadequate when she is out of her element. And a restaurant like this one is not something she experiences often. But for now, the young lady feels enchanted by the grand atmosphere. The moon shines down on her for extra warmth and comfort. Her heart is jubilant and zealous.

As Raj approaches, somewhat out of breath, Anika calls out to him. "Listen, body, this is Mumbai. You need to stay alert, or you'll miss the train."

Raj replies, smiling. "It's not 'body,' it's 'buddy.' "

Anika gives a laugh. "Whatever. Let's get inside. You must be hungry now that you've had your second exercise of the day."

The Marker

The expansive lobby to the restaurant is plain but elegant. A large red rug hugs the floor of the logia. The floor covering is intricate in its design. Green and yellow florals snake through its fabric. Every stitch of the masterpiece is set with perfection. It is a silk rug, handwoven from Kashmir, and it gives the impression that it once comforted the feet of royalty.

A solo violinist, dressed in a tuxedo with a red bow tie, plays towards the far corner. The musician is playing Carl Maria Van Weber's Violin Sonata Opus 10. The ambiance that it creates is light and airy, yet refined and proper, but not fastidious.

A young male, likely a teenager, attends a small cloakroom. The small room sits past the front door, towards the left of the entryway.

"Don't disappear, Uncle," Anika says as she steps away to the ladies' room at the far end of the lobby.

Raj waits by the entrance. He notices a medium-sized, silver-plated bowl on a small antique table to the right of the doorway. On the table, behind the dish, is a sign that reads, "Kindly deposit your mobile here. Enjoy your dinner!"

Raj opens the drawer to the antique table and finds a marker inside. He looks around him and observes that he is alone. Raj then rubs away the word 'mobile' from the sign with his hand and replaces it with the word 'brain.' He then returns the marker to its place in the drawer. Raj then turns his attention to the cloakroom, where its attendant greets him. "Hello, Uncle! Welcome to the Maharaja Café."

Raj is somewhat offended. "Uncle?" Raj leans in towards the teenager and notices his nametag, which says, "SRK." Raj continues in a heated tone. "Listen, SRK..."

SRK interrupts. "Relax, old man! At least I didn't call you Grandpa."

Raj feels chagrined. "How about I..."

The attendant interrupts again. "Hey, just because you're out to eat with a young lady doesn't make you any younger."

Exasperation consumes Raj's countenance. Raj is about to respond again when Anika returns from the ladies' room. She notices that Raj is angry with the attendant, but she doesn't know why. Yet, she proceeds to grab Raj's hand and, with a smile, pulls him towards the dining area.

"Come on, Uncle, let's go eat."

SRK laughs upon hearing Anika call Raj 'Uncle,' but there's nothing Raj can do at this point. Raj follows Anika with obedience into the dining room, his head lowered.

The Glasses

The dining area is lavish and stylish, but not too ornate. The tables are set far apart, and almost all the tables are full of patrons. Each place setting has a multitude of high-quality glasses, silverware, and plates.

Most of the male guests are wearing jackets and ties, and most of the female guests are wearing fancy *saris*. Instrumental music, accompanied by another solo violinist fills the air. Raj and Anika sit at a table towards the far corner of the room, near a window.

Raj peers out the window and up towards the sky.

"What do you see outside?" the young lady inquires.

"Not much, actually. I was counting the stars."

"Oh, why is that?"

"You said this place has eight stars. I only count three."

She places her hands on her hips, fists closed. "Listen, body."

Raj replies, smiling, "It's not 'body,' it's 'buddy.'"

Anika gives a laugh. "Whatever."

Three waiters, also dressed in tuxedos but with black bowties, line up towards the right of their table. The first one steps towards the table. He hands a drink menu to Anika and another one to Raj. "Would you like to begin with a cocktail, madam?"

"No, thank you."

The waiter picks up the cocktail glass from the table.

"Champagne for you?" the first waiter now asks.

"No, thank you," Anika replies again.

The waiter picks up the champagne glass from the table.

"How about white wine?" he asks.

"No, thank you."

The waiter picks up the white wine glass from the table.

"Red?"

"No, thank you."

The waiter picks up the red wine glass from the table.

Finally, only a water glass remains. "Why so many glasses?" Raj asks the first waiter. "Do most customers have six types of liquor with dinner?"

Before the waiter can respond, Anika chimes in, "It's a standard custom, Uncle Raj. The more glasses, the more stars for the restaurant." She then addresses the first waiter. "I'll have a chocolate martini, please."

"Fine choice," the waiter says. "And for you, sir? Would you like to begin with a cocktail?"

Raj holds up his hand. "I'll just have a KF."

"Very well, sir." The waiter proceeds to remove the rest of the glasses from the table.

As the waiter is doing this, the young lady asks, "KF?"

"I never order beer, only KF... Kingfisher," Raj explains.

Anika nods back with an understanding smile.

The first waiter leaves to get the drinks. The second waiter, holding a silver tray with a wooden box and two menus, approaches the table. The second waiter hands an appetizer menu to the young lady, and then he gives the other to Raj. He then leans towards Raj and opens the wooden box for him. Inside the wooden box are four reading glasses of varying levels of thickness.

This offends Raj. He has perfect vision and no need for visual support. "Excuse me, what's your name?"

"Sir, my name is Dhansukh." Noticing that he has offended his customer, the waiter continues. "Sir, this is a standard custom. Some of our elderly clients prefer…"

Raj's temper flares. "Elderly?! I would like to speak to your manager. I have a few words for him."

Dhansukh steps away in compliance, and the manager returns (also wearing a tuxedo, but with a gold bow tie). He appears to be Dhansukh's twin brother. "Hello, sir, my name is Mansukh. How may I help you?"

"Listen," Raj begins, "just because I have a few grey hairs doesn't mean I'm too old to read a menu."

"Sir, this is a standard custom," Mansukh responds. "Some of our elderly clients prefer…"

Fumes begin to rise from Raj's mostly black hair. "I find it troubling that you assume my health is failing."

"Raj," Anika interrupts, "there's nothing wrong with reading glasses. I use them myself." Anika takes out a pair of reading glasses from her purse and puts them on her face. While reviewing the menu in front of her, she continues. "If you need them, use them. One day you might make a huge mistake if you cannot see well enough. Pride cannot fix a genetic disposition. It can only mask it."

Raj, unable to argue with the young lady's logic, nods the manager away. Dhansukh returns. "Appetizers for the table?"

The items on the appetizer menu have long, fancy, almost incomprehensible names. Anika points to the second item. "Dhansukh, how's this one?"

"Excellent choice, madam," the waiter replies. "It's a Maharaja specialty. It's a carefully baked item with a savoury filling. The dish includes finely spiced and perfectly cubed King Edward potatoes, jubilantly cut red, white, and yellow onions, tossed with early perfection peas, and French green lentils. To this, we add a hint of pine nuts, and we assemble the item in the shape of a tetrahedral pastry."

"You mean *samosas*?" Anika responds.

"Yes, madam," says the waiter.

Raj points to the last item. "Dhansukh, how about this one?"

"Excellent choice, sir. It's a Maharaja specialty. This signature dish features delicately diced Opperdoeszer Ronde potatoes, mixed with farm-fresh spring onions and a delicate blend of organic *turmeric, garam masala*, and cumin seeds hand-dipped in gluten-free chickpea flour. The blend is then fried to perfection and served with a garnish of finely chopped coriander and air-dried fenugreek leaves."

"You mean *pakoras*?" Anika questions.

"Okay, let's go with the *samosas* and *pakoras*," Raj affirms.

"Excellent choices. I'll put the order in right away," Dhansukh avows as he collects the appetizer menus from the couple.

The third waiter steps up to the table and hands a dinner menu to Anika and another to Raj.

Dhansukh returns to the kitchen. He calls out the order to the cook, loud enough so that the diners can hear him, as the door swings back open behind him. "Order for table four. Chef, microwave more of those *samosas* and *pakoras* from the freezer right away."

Raj, being a vegetarian, finds little choice on the menu. "Any vegetarian specials for today?" he inquires the third waiter.

"No, sir, we have chicken *korma* and lamb *biryani* for you."

"But I'm vegetarian," Raj replies. "Are you saying that you don't have any vegetarian specials?"

"No, sir. How about our chicken *korma*? Our lamb *biryani* is also very nice."

"Who is running this place exactly? Let me speak to him."

"That would be our father, Sukh Sukh. Would you like me to get him?"

"Forget it," Raj replies, understanding the hopelessness of the situation.

A Non-Resident Indian (NRI) couple occupies the table next to Anika's. An NRI is an Indian that lives outside of the country. Many NRIs try to visit their mother country every few years, like this husband and wife. The husband and wife are elderly and likely retired. Both are overweight, and both are wearing a frown as if unsatisfied by the quality of the air in the restaurant.

Anika and Raj both overhear the NRI wife ordering the couple's dinner: "We would like bottled water, no ice. And one chutney sandwich. But no green cucumbers, no lettuce, and no chutney."

"Very well, madam," her waiter responds. "Would you like anything else with your bread?"

"No butter," she barks.

The third waiter turns his attention back towards Raj. "That's typical of NRIs. Always worried about getting sick. Fortunately, our bread's the best in Mumbai. Sir, may I recommend the lamb *biriyani* for you? We can substitute the lamb with vegetables."

"Sure," grumbles Raj.

"I'll have the chicken vindaloo." Anika points to the second item on the menu.

"Excellent choices. I'll put the order right away," the third waiter responds, stepping away to the kitchen. The third waiter belts out to the chef: "Two more frozen dinners, Chef—one lamb *biriyani*, one chicken vindaloo. Toss the lamb out, though. Table four."

The Passion

The appetizers arrive, along with the chocolate martini and the King Fisher. They could have put together the same items for themselves after a quick trip to the Seven-Eleven. Even so, Raj and Anika enjoy the starters.

"They should get Ramla to work here. The appetizers last night were incredible," Raj notes.

Anika shakes her head left and right, "No way, Mister. I can't live without Ramla. I would starve without him."

"Cheers! To the real cook. Ramla, the master chef," Raj holds up his beer bottle.

"Cheers! I second that," Anika smiles. And after a pause, she continues the conversation. "Uncle Raj, how do you keep busy in Goa?"

"Well, there's the hotel, among other things. It's currently offseason, but we still have plenty of guests."

"Wow, it must be fun. Do you get to meet lots of interesting travellers?"

"I do, in fact. For the most part, it's vacationers looking to get away from their busy city lives. We pride ourselves on excellent service, supreme comfort, and tranquillity."

"How do you manage it all, especially when you're traveling?" Anika wonders.

"To tell you the truth, this is the first time I've left home in over two decades," Raj considers as he rubs his chin.

"Are you serious? You must have been really busy."

"Yes. Busy is good. 'Better get busy living, or get busy dying,' " Raj observes.

"That sounds like it's straight from a movie," the young lady snickers.

"Ha. No idea. My father used to say that. No idea where he got it from though. But I like to keep busy. And I've always believed that it's better to do a few things well, rather than do many things poorly. So for this second half of my life, I've devoted all my efforts to my family's affairs. After my father passed away, I felt it my duty to carry on his life's efforts."

"Uncle, I'm in awe. That is incredibly inspiring. Is there someone special in your life, someone who has helped you through all this?" the young lady inquires, with a hinting expression.

"Yes, there is." Raj gives a blank response.

Anika's eyes widen, and she holds her breath as she searches his face for more information. Then after a moment, she calls out, "Well, tell me more silly."

"I have my good friend, my brother, in fact, taking charge for me right now," Raj reveals.

"Wait, you have a brother? Daddy said you were an only child." Anika is even more surprised.

"Technically, I am. But my father adopted a baby boy. I think I was about five years old at the time when my father had just started his first business."

Anika feels elated and charmed. "Tell me about your brother. I want to know all about him."

"His name is Ram Iqbal. He's my closest confidant. I trust him more than anyone. I've never met a more honest and humble human. Ram Iqbal is taking constant care of things while I'm gone, I'm sure."

"How did Ram Iqbal come to meet your family?"

"He just showed up when he was a baby."

"Babies don't just show up," replies the young lady in a questioning tone.

"This one did," Raj insists.

"Did Ram Iqbal just show up in an Uber one day?" Anika chortles.

"No, we didn't have Uber back then. Ram Iqbal showed up one day at the doorstep of the hospital a few months after he was born. No one knew his name, his parents, or where he came from. And of course, no one knew his religion—Hindu or Muslim. So, they named the baby Ram Iqbal."

"That makes sense. Incredible. Ram Iqbal, what an awesome name as well!" Anika beams.

"But the baby's new name didn't help his fate, at least not at first. No Indian would take the baby in, given that Iqbal is an Islamic name. And no Muslim would take the baby in, given that Ram is a Hindu name. It turned into a real mess."

"Poor thing. But that wasn't even the baby's real name," she replies, now saddened.

He continues. "It didn't matter in the eyes of the townspeople, and given that our town was small, we didn't even have an orphanage. The elders in our town met, and my father was one of them. Nobody wanted to take responsibility for the baby, and the hospital couldn't keep him forever. Most wanted to drop him off on the doorstep of some other town's hospital. My father wouldn't have it that way. He took the baby in that very day, and Ram Iqbal has been living with my family ever since."

The young lady's countenance is full of intrigue. "I do have one question," she adds, with hesitation in her voice.

"Fire away."

"Well, what happens if he were to die? Will Ram Iqbal be cremated per Hindu custom, or will he be buried per Muslim custom?"

"I hope that I never have to face that day. But if so, we'll just leave it up to the media and the politicians to decide," Raj chuckles, with a smile.

They both laugh at this.

"I actually happen to know Ram Iqbal's actual desire," Raj continues. "He doesn't want to be cremated or buried. Ram Iqbal plans on donating his remains to medical research."

"That's really noble. I would love to meet Ram Iqbal one day."

"How about now?"

Raj reaches for his pocket but realizes that he left his phone in the bowl near the entrance. "Here, hand me your phone."

She opens her purse and takes out her phone. The young lady passes her phone to Raj, and he sends a quick text to Ram: "Raj to Ram Iqbal. How's the home base?"

They wait a few moments, but the brother does not reply. Still, Anika saves his number in her phone in case he does. At this point, dinner arrives, and the two begin eating again.

"How's the chicken?" inquires Raj.

"Tastes like mutton, actually." Anika swallows and then responds with a frown.

"That's strange. So does my *biryani*. Let's hope the dessert doesn't taste like mutton as well," Raj chortles. Then after taking a sip of his KF, "So young lady, how do you keep busy these days?"

At this point, Anika puts down her fork and knife and gives a contemplative stare out the window. She takes a shallow breath, and then utters back in response, "To be honest. Not much lately."

"Really? Your mother told me that you volunteer at the orphanage."

"Well, I guess. But I haven't been lately." The young lady looks back out the window, and she becomes lost in thought. "Uncle Raj, can I ask you something?"

"Shoot."

"How did you find your passion?"

Raj takes another bite of his dinner, and then another sip of his KF. Then after placing it back down, he replies. "I will be candid with you. It took me a long time to figure this out. And you likely won't hear this from others as it is not a common belief. But I have a different view on passion than most people."

"Oh, yeah? I would love to hear what you have to say about it."

"Well, it is my opinion that passion is completely overrated."

This shocks the young lady, as she did not expect such a response.

Raj continues, "Too many people search for passion, and then they give up too quickly. Simply because life is not that exciting and interesting all the time. Life is challenging. Life is frustrating. Life is suffering. Life is even boring. And those that search for passion are likely to get disappointed by these facts."

"So then what motivates you?" Anika takes a sip of her martini.

"It's the simple things. Like enjoying a good meal." He motions to his plate. "Or enjoying good company." He picks up his KF and points the open end at the young lady. "Or simply working hard, and not expecting anything else in return."

The young lady sits back in her chair, and she crosses her hands on her lap. She then rubs her elbows as if she's scratching an itch that appeared on each arm at the same time. And while Anika does this, she looks towards the heavens for gratitude, but she is not sure why. "That's certainly a different perspective on things," she replies at last.

After another sip of his drink, Raj continues, "In fact, the best motivator in my life is helping others. I find when I'm helping other people, I become less troubled by my own problems. And as my father would say, 'the best way to become less selfish is to act selflessly.' "

"You sure did learn a bunch from your father." Anika feels exalted by the conversation. She did not expect to have such a profound discussion over dinner. The young lady takes another sip of her drink to wash down her last bite of food, and then she asks, "So, what did he mean by that?"

"What he meant is that all too often we end up brooding and tormenting ourselves. We cling to what we 'could' and 'should' be doing. But the best way to escape these harmful, unproductive thoughts... these selfish thoughts, is to be selfless. Meaning to help others. Like how you help those children at the orphanage."

"Right." The young lady gives a flat response.

"So, when you're helping others, you forget about your own troubles. Makes sense?"

"Yes. It does." This deluge of information is far more than the young lady had anticipated over a meal. But she is grateful for the opportunity to learn from someone with such a different perspective on life. And so she feels resplendent. So after another sip of her martini, Anika looks at Raj in the eyes and gives him a sweet smile, "Thank you."

"The pleasure is all mine, Anika. To share what I have learned with just one person means the world to me. I mean it. Cheers!" He picks up his KF and taps it against her raised martini.

"Cheers!" she gushes back.

The Nightcap

Next up is dessert. It is a lemon tart. But it is only about the size of a rupee coin. And it rests on an oversized plate, with chocolate syrup drizzled all about the plate and the tart. The waiter places the grand plate in the centre of the table with care. He then puts one tiny wooden spoon in front of Raj, and another similar spoon in front of Anika. The tart turns out to be very yummy.

The couple finishes eating, and Raj pays the bill with the gift card. The third waiter returns. "Sir, you still have funds remaining on the gift card. Would you and your lady care for a coffee or drink in our lounge?"

Raj turns towards Anika, and she gives an approving nod. "Sounds like a plan," Raj gives him a thumbs up.

An elegant, old-fashioned table rests at the far end of the lounge. The table is cedar, and it is hand carved with intricate designs resembling the likes of a Hindu temple. And on top of the table rests a wide assortment of cakes, pastries, and Indian sweets.

The desserts are bite-sized, like the tart they had for dessert. But these desserts lie on small, tiny plates with gold leaf around the edge of each dish. Miniature shots of already pored liquor, dessert wine, and coffee liquor surround the sweets.

"Uncle Raj, you pick first," the young lady begins.

"Sure, what's your favourite colour?" he inquires.

"Mauve."

"Is that so?"

"But more of a pastel mauve—not too bright, just a light purple," Anika explains.

Raj picks up a red velvet shortcake with blue icing and hands it to Anika. "Here, try this one."

"Wait, that's not mauve."

"Well, purple is not a true colour; it's not even on the rainbow. Your brain only picks up red, blue, and green. And when your brain sees red and blue close together, it makes up a colour for it—purple."

Anika is sceptical, but she takes the red velvet cake and eats it in one bite. "Okay, what's your favourite colour?"

"Green."

She hands him a tiny cup filled with a creamy violet mousse, with green whipped cream on top. "Here, try this."

Raj takes the tiny spoon from the little cup and consumes the mousse with genuine joy. "Okay, what's your favourite animal?" he asks.

"Cuttlefish."

Raj picks up a tiny strawberry creampuff and hands it to Anika. "Here, try this one."

She devours the bite-sized cake in one go. "Yum. Okay, what's your favourite animal?"

"Bonobos."

"Never heard of them," Anika squints her eyes as if pondering the name of the animal will conjure up a mental image.

The couple goes back and forth a few times, and soon, many small plates pile up in front of them both. The two are feeling a little high and a bit boisterous.

The first waiter comes over. "Ah, I see you found our alcoholic dessert section," he says, pointing to the sign above the table.

Raj and Anika stare back at each other, at first, a little confused. And then they both burst out laughing at the same time.

The first waiter continues. "Would you like a nightcap or how about a coffee?"

"Coffee!" Raj and Anika respond in unison.

The Bonfire

Back at the coatroom, SRK slumps over the counter. Anika and Raj walk towards the exit, arm-in-arm.

"How was dinner, sir?" SRK inquires with a broad smile on his face.

Raj replies, trying not to smile too much, "Good."

"Splendid," the young lady chimes in, half giggling.

"Here's your phone. I upgraded your music library," SRK says. The attendant then hands back Raj's phone.

Raj gets angry for a moment. "You what?"

"Relax, Uncle. Calm down. These songs are from your generation. I'm sure you'll like them."

Raj looks over the phone and sees that the attendant has downloaded many of his favourite oldies onto the phone.

"I see," Raj replies, now smiling.

"It charged your account a hundred rupees for the 250 songs." SRK grins.

Raj plays the first song. He then puts the phone in the front pocket of his shirt. He then takes out a tip from his wallet and hands the cash over the counter. "Well done, SRK. Please order us a limo taxi."

"As you wish," the attendant replies.

SRK picks up the phone in his booth and speaks a few words. And less than a few seconds later, a fancy Audi convertible pulls up in front of the restaurant. Both Raj and Anika look surprised and gleeful.

"Hey, Uncle, now that we have a nice ride, how about we hit the town?" the young lady suggests.

"Let's do it. SRK, when do you finish?" Raj asks.

"Sir, you're our last guest."

"Great, you can be our DJ. Hop in," Raj feels gregarious, but he is also drunk.

All three jump into the car—SRK in front, and Anika and Raj in the back. The Audi speeds off.

Late that night, the car, once spotless and polished, is now dusty and half covered in mud (for some unknown reason). The car pulls into the carport of the Malhotras. Once home, the young lady stumbles out from the left door and Raj out the right.

At this point, their minds are buzzing, but their bodies feel exhausted. Anika thinks that they must have been to a concert, but Raj insists that they were at a club. Both recall a bonfire on the beach, but neither remembers the ice cream after. Either way, the evening was full of more excitement than either had anticipated.

"Goodnight, lady," Raj manages to say, eyes half-closed.

"Night, mister," Anika replies, eyes also half-closed.

Anika and Raj both turn towards the car and wave goodbye. "Goodnight, SRK!" they both shout.

She heads towards the entrance of the house, and he towards the pool house and the Audi drives off.

The Paan

The next morning, Mangla wakes up early and begins her morning routine. Although she is in her late fifties, she is a very modern woman. The woman may be the family's head maid, but she embraces technology like a teenager. She also loves learning about new scientific findings the moment they come out. Mangla even has a subscription to Nature and Science and many other publications.

Her husband of the same age is the complete opposite. Ramla is old fashioned. He has the same hairstyle that a barber gave him when he was ten years old. And he still visits the same barber to this day. He always prefers the safest, most traditional approach. This is especially true when it comes to critical life choices.

Mangla puts on her Bluetooth headphones and listens to urban-classical mixes. At the same time, she reads the latest headlines from Science.com. She comes across an article about a study involving married couples. The research finds that texting positive messages each day to partners increases marital satisfaction.

After spending some time catching up on the world's latest discoveries, she opens up an app on her phone. The app is 'Spanish in 20 Days.'

"Dónde está la comida?" she says out loud as she heads towards the closet. "La comida está allí." While Mangla is getting ready, she texts her husband, who is still sleeping in the bed.

Mangla's text reads: "Get up, dear. I miss your smile."

Ramla wakes up to the sound of his phone, receiving a new message. He is in a dream state, and without his glasses, he cannot make out the text message. Why is Meena texting me so early? He thinks to himself. Sometimes, if Meena invites a guest over at the last minute, Ramla will receive a text so that he can prepare. The chef can whip up a great meal with his eyes closed, but his best work takes preparation.

Mangla is now inside the closet, and she sends another text message to her husband, who is still half-asleep. The new text reads: "I [heart] you."

"Yo quiero arroz con pollo," the maid calls out to herself.

Ramla hears his wife, but he doesn't understand her command. "Meena wants *puri*?"

"Dónde está la comida?" Mangla continues her lesson.

Confusion festers inside Ramla's mind. He scratches his head and inquires to his wife, "Meena wants *paan*? This early?"

"La comida está allí," the wife calls out again.

"Mr. Ali is coming? Oh my, I'll make the *paan*, right away." The husband jumps out of bed, throws on his pants and shirt, and leaves for the kitchen.

Ramla stumbles into the kitchen, but he finds it empty. Still confused, he looks back at his phone. The husband finally realizes that the text wasn't from Meena, but rather, it was Mangla.

"Useless phones," the chef mumbles to himself as he begins to prep the kitchen for breakfast.

The Internet

Breakfast is ready, and Raj and Prakash are sitting on one side of the breakfast table. Meena is reading the morning paper on the other side.

Anika meanders, half asleep, into the room. "Smells great, Ramla! You're always up bright and early, aren't you?"

The chef has his back to the breakfast table, and he grunts in response. "Yeah, that's right."

The daughter takes a seat next to her mother. She reaches across the table and grabs a grape from the fruit bowl near the centre and places it in her mouth. Anika looks happy, but she seems tired and a bit hung over.

Meena looks up from her paper with a slight frown. "You look sleepy, young lady. When did you get in?"

"Yeah, we ended up staying up late at the library. We had to do some important research," Anika gives a soft chuckle.

"Oh yeah? What were you researching?" the mother asks, egging her on.

The young lady says the first thing that comes to her mind. She hopes that her mother will drop the line of questioning. "We were doing some last-minute research on African primates."

"Oh yeah? Which primates?" Meena inquires, not expecting an answer to her previous question.

Anika responds with a half-smile and now looking in the direction of Raj. "Bonobos. They're one of the world's most peaceful primates. They're the only primate who has figured out how to avoid murder, war, and bloodshed. Do you know how, Mama?"

The mother was not expecting a rational, cogent response. All Meena can do is look back at her daughter, half impressed and half confused. "No, I don't. Tell me."

The daughter continues, now looking back at her mother. "It's because, with bonobos, the females are in charge. If any male starts to act out, the females team up against the aggressive male."

Prakash interrupts, knowing fully well that Anika and Raj were out late having a good time. "I'm glad to hear that you're keeping on top of your studies, Anika. But I have an important announcement to make."

"What's that, dear?" asks the wife.

"I'm retiring and planning to become a *Bollywood* actor."

"What?" The entire room, including Ramla, responds at the same time.

"Yes, I start auditions next week. I'm aiming for best supporting actor."

The room is silent, and all attention is on the patriarch.

"I'm kidding," the father continues. "Listen, Meena and Anika, in all seriousness, I have some important news."

The mother and daughter give their undivided attention to Prakash, and he continues. "We have a boy that is interested in seeing you, Anika."

Anika's smile evaporates.

The father keeps going. "The boy is the nephew of a physician that I work with at the hospital. The physician is a Parsi but was born and raised in Mumbai. His brother is Rustom Darwajawala, a retired lawyer. Rustom's son, Billu Darwajawala, would very much like to meet you, Anika."

"Why would I want to meet him?" Anika asks.

"Well, he's a computer genius," Prakash replies.

The young lady responds in haste, somewhat agitated. "Daddy, there's nothing wrong with our internet. There's no need, I assure you."

The father is now frowning. "Anika, he's not coming to fix our broadband. Listen, give him a chance."

"He's a Parsi and a lawyer?" Meena chimes in.

The father, feeling defensive, responds. "Yes, Rustom's a lawyer, but he's never practiced law; he's a wealthy landlord and a good man."

Anika responds, with a defensive tone. "Okay, if I ever need any legal advice about my hard drive, I'll be sure to give Rustom and Billu a call. Sounds good, Daddy?"

The young lady is open to meeting boys. Or at least she thinks she is. Still, Anika is reluctant when it comes to potential matches picked by her father. In the past, he has focused on traits that he would like to see in a son-in-law. But Anika always felt that her father did not give much consideration to her desires.

Given past experience, Prakash expects pushback. "Listen, everyone, relax. There's nothing wrong with just seeing the boy. He's a smart kid. Although he's never finished high school, he's very good at computers. He's super talented."

"You need to work on your sales pitch, Daddy," the daughter responds.

"Prakash," the mother chimes in, "are you sure this is the right time?"

The father gets annoyed, and his frustration begins to show in his demeanour. "Listen, my decision is final. The boy is coming this evening, and we will greet him and his father with kindness and respect."

Meena capitulates, turning towards the chef. "Ramla, please prepare some snacks for our guests."

Ramla grumbles again in the background. "In my day, the daughter would not even be told until the wedding day. Those were simpler times," he thinks to himself.

At this point, Raj gives out a big laugh. "Maybe he can fix the email on my phone?"

The young lady places her hands on her hips, fists closed, and gives Raj a stern glare. "Listen, body."

The guest replies, smiling, "It's not 'body,' it's 'buddy.' "

"Whatever," she gives a curt reply.

The Son

It is now evening, and Anika sits on her living room couch, reading a non-fiction hardcover, *The Science of Color*, by Steven K. Shevell. She wears a simple, yellow *sari* and no makeup. Her hair is down and pulled to the side. Prakash is reading the Wall Street Journal, and Meena is watering her flowers.

Rustom and Billu arrive, and Prakash and Meena greet them at the door. Rustom is a rotund fellow. He has a prominent chin, a thick beard, and a jolly countenance, and he wears a purple, velvet tracksuit. Billu, skinny and thin, is wearing jeans and a black t-shirt. The young man has a flat nose and short, black hair, parted to the right. Thick-rimmed, black glasses sit upon his narrow face.

The father shakes Rustom's squishy hand and then Billu's frail hand. "Welcome, welcome. Do come on in."

The mother gives a slight bow. "*Namaste*."

"Thank you, Doctor," Rustom says. "A pleasure to meet you. This is Billu. Son, kneel at the elders' feet for their blessings, will you?"

The young man shrugs his shoulders and then proceeds to put his forehead down, and he raises his legs up. Before he can complete his headstand, Rustom yanks his son up. In an annoyed voice, Rustom continues. "That'll be all, boy. Stand back up."

They all walk in towards the living room.

"This is my daughter," Prakash announces, turning towards the young lady. "Anika, this is Rustom and his son, Billu."

Anika stands and gives a slight bow. "Pleased to meet you both."

"Hello, dear," Rustom gives a small wave. He then turns towards Prakash. "Why don't we let the boy and girl get to know each other in private?"

"Yes, yes," Prakash agrees. "Great idea. Sughandha, take Anika and Billu to the den so that they can talk in private."

The Coffee

The den is a simple room filled with white wicker furniture. It has two French doors that connect to the living room. To the left is an armchair, to the right is a love seat, to the centre is a couch, and in between is a coffee table. Two large windows behind the sofa envelope the room with sunshine. Orchids fill the air with a fresh scent, and other houseplants provide a lush ambiance.

On the far wall, opposite the French doors, rest portraits of Anika's grandparents. Both of her grandmothers and grandfathers have passed away. But Anika goes into the den from time to time to visit them and pay her respects.

Anika was especially close to her grandmother on her father's side. She called this grandmother Nun Nani, and it was this grandmother who helped raise her when she was young. Anika has fond memories of Nun Nani walking with her to and from her grade school. Nani would enjoy reading to Anika. And Anika would enjoy listening to Nani's old tales, like how her father used to run away from the table as a young boy whenever he did not want to finish his vegetables. But also, it was Nani that would defend Anika whenever she disagreed with her father.

In secondary school, Anika wanted to play football, but Prakash was more than reluctant. Her father had seen too many students with concussions enter the emergency room from the sport. "The girl's team is rougher than the boys even. What a reckless sport!"

"Let her live!" Nun Nani would scold her son. Prakash was stubborn, but Nun Nani was the only one who could stand up to him.

After they enter, Billu takes a seat in the armchair. And Anika sits in the loveseat on the opposite side of the coffee table. For a few moments, they stare at each other without saying anything. The young lady then looks over at Nun Nani and makes a small prayer. "Please save me from this torture," the young lady whispers to herself.

She then turns back towards Billu and gives him an icy glare. The young man has yet to say a word to Anika. He looks straight at the young lady, but it is as if he is staring right through her. Billu's expression is vacant, and he seems to be lost in thought.

After a few minutes, Anika breaks the silence. "Did you grow up around here?"

"Yes, I did, in fact."

More silence.

Anika breaks the silence again. "What do you do for fun?"

"Well, I like AI."

More silence.

After a while, he continues. "It means Artificial Intelligence."

"I know what AI means," Anika snaps back.

More silence.

Anika breaks the silence yet again. "Have you done much traveling lately?"

"Yes, we went to Juhu Beach this morning."

More silence.

"Okay, Billu. How about you ask me a question?"

Billu thinks for a moment and then finally responds. "What's your name?"

At this point, Anika has had enough. "Billu, how about we go back and join the rest of them? Would you like some coffee?"

"Oh yes," Billu responds without hesitation, "I love coffee! Do you have Starbucks?"

Anika rolls her eyes, stands up, and walks out the door.

The Cable

Anika and Billu make their way back to the living room. Anika is in front, and she takes swift strides to outpace the young man, who trails behind with his head down. The young lady enters the living room first. She makes eye contact with her mother without the others noticing. Anika frowns and gives her mother the 'thumbs down.'

Meena immediately springs into action. "Welcome back, you two! Well, the two of you must have a lot to think about. Prakash, we're heading to dinner soon. Should we let our guests be on their way?"

Before Prakash can reply, Meena continues. "I want to thank you both for stopping by, and we look forward to the next time we can meet again." While she's saying this, she ushers Rustom and Billu out the door.

The abrupt departure confuses Rustom, so he looks towards his son for some insight.

"Are we all going to Starbucks now?" Billu inquires.

Back in the house, Anika sits on the couch. She feels somewhat relieved, but also vindicated. Prakash is contrite and apologetic. "Frankly, I'm shocked. I was expecting something entirely different."

Meena takes this opportunity to retort. "Prakash, I don't know what you were thinking. You really need to talk to me first before subjecting our daughter to this kind of situation."

At this point, Raj returns from playing tennis with Ramu. He is quick to realize that the evening's visitors didn't leave a great impression on the family.

Raj tries to ease the tension in the room and turns towards Prakash. "Come on, old friend, let's grab a beer on the patio."

Meanwhile, Ramu runs into the father-and-son duo at the gate to the house. Ramu is also dressed in a tennis outfit, but he is sweating far more than Raj was.

Ramu walks up to the Rustom and Billu. "Great, you must be here to fix our cable. Can you also sign us up for HBO?"

Rustom and Billu give each other a confused look. Billu shrugs his shoulders. "Would you also like ESPN?"

Rustom becomes agitated, and he grabs Billu by the shoulder and pushes him out of the gate. Ramu gives a confused look. But he is quick to brush it off. The chauffeur proceeds to walk back towards the house, humming the theme to the Price Is Right.

The Dress

A few days later, everything is back to normal it seems, or at least back to how things were before the Billu affair. Anika and Raj return from their morning jog, which has now become a part of their daily routine.

"You hardly broke a sweat today, Uncle," Anika says. "Is the trail too easy for you now?"

"It's perfect for me," Raj huffs as he begins to get his breath back. "Fresh air, beautiful scenery, and something to get my heart pumping. That's all I need from my morning run."

From out of nowhere, the young lady brings up Billu's visit. "I can't believe my father would try to hook me up with some random boy."

Raj is a bit taken aback. "He does have your best interests at heart, Anika."

"I know. It's not Daddy's best interests that I'm worried about. It's his approach."

"Maybe he learned a thing or two from this last time."

"I truly hope so. I can't imagine having to go through something like that again."

"Have you ever thought of trying to find someone on your own?"

"Perhaps. I need to hang out where the cool kids hang out."

"Now, you're thinking. What's your plan?"

Anika thinks for a moment and then responds. "I have my cousin's party in a few weeks. He's graduating from university and throwing a big event. Maybe I'll meet someone there? Wouldn't that be great, Uncle Raj? Then this whole mess can be put to rest once and for all."

"See, all it takes is a bit of imagination. It's not as bad as you think."

Anika appears to be enthralled. "Great, it's settled. I'm going this afternoon to get a dress for the special event. Come with me shopping. We'll grab ice cream after."

"Sounds like a plan, Anika!"

Ramu accompanies Anika and Raj to a designer boutique after lunch. The establishment specializes in custom, high-end dresses. The showroom sits between an art gallery and a coffee shop. The boutique is also surrounded by many other high-end stores. Yet, most of the shops are empty.

As Ramu, Anika, and Raj enter, three attendants greet them before the doorman can close the door. The first attendant, a young man, serves the three patrons *chai*. The second attendant, a young lady in a purple *sari*, sits the three shoppers on chairs facing a massive wall of mirrors. Anika sits in the middle, Ramu sits to her left, and Raj to her right.

And the third attendant, an old man with a white moustache, begins to bring out wedding dresses. The old man is the tailor, and he is wearing a bleached-white collared dress shirt with tidy black pants.

"No, these are way too fancy," Anika frowns.

"But you only get married once, my dear," the tailor winks at Raj.

"I'm not getting married. Like I said, I just want something that sparkles for a party."

"Your reception? No problem madam." The elderly man scurries to the back and comes back with two lavish dresses on each arm.

"Maybe this old man needs his hearing checked?" Ramu chuckles to Anika.

"These two are from our Sapphire Collection. Your guests will be enchanted, I'm sure. Only the best for your daughter, right?" The tailor gives a big smile to Ramu.

The chauffeur cannot help but snicker, "You can't argue with that."

Anika looks at Ramu and gives a frustrated sigh. She then stands up and walks right past the tailor and heads to the backroom by herself.

"But madam, I'm more than happy to bring the items to you," as the old man chases after her.

Over the next hour, Anika proceeds to try on dresses of all different styles. But more suited to her taste. Raj, Ramu, and the tailor give their votes (thumbs up and thumbs down). For the most part, all three judges cannot agree.

Meanwhile, a lady in her mid-forties, portly but well-dressed, approaches Raj. "Uncle, I'm interested in the dress from the showcase. Do you have one I can try on?"

Raj once again does not like the fact that someone called him 'Uncle,' and he gives the lady a curt reply, "Uncle?"

"Yes, Uncle," the rotund lady continues, "can you help me out with that dress?"

"I'm sorry, madam," Raj counters, "but that is simply not possible."

A look of dismay engulfs the lady's face. She has the attitude of a royal heiress that always gets her way. "And why not, may I ask?"

"You don't want to know, madam."

The lady pushes back. "Tell me. I demand to know."

"Sorry, but there's no way a dress like that would fit you."

The lady is now fuming. "What did you say?"

"It's against store policy to let someone try on a dress that is too small to fit," Raj counters.

The rotund lady opens her mouth wide as if she was singing an opera, but instead, she yells, "Never in my life!"

Anika is changing back into her original clothing. And she overhears the erupting argument outside of her change room. She cannot help but laugh to herself. Even so, the young lady is rapid to get dressed and make a swift exit.

As Raj is about to respond again, Anika grabs him by the arm and pulls him out of the store.

Ramu heads out the door behind them, but before he leaves, he tells the lady, "I'm sorry, lady. We'll have more in stock next week. Come back then."

The lady is more confused than angry at this point. But she has no one to direct her confusion and anger towards, as everyone around her has disappeared.

The Uncle

A few days later, Ramu is cleaning the car in the driveway, and Meena is watering the plants in the garden. She is wearing a sun hat made of light wicker. It has a wide brim and an ornate border. And the hat matches her garden apron and her garden gloves. Three-piece set was a Mother's Day gift from her daughter many years ago, and even though the mother uses it often, it looks new.

Ramu calls out to Meena, "Perfect day, isn't it, Madam?"

Meena puts down her water pitcher and approaches the chauffeur. "It is. Ramu, can I ask you something?"

He puts the soapy rag down and looks up at the matriarch. "Yes, of course, madam. How can I help you?"

She is apprehensive but proceeds anyway. "What happened to the dress? Anika said something about having to run out of the store, but she wouldn't give me any details."

"Nothing really. Raj was practicing his customer service skills. It didn't go so well."

Meena gives a confused look and continues with reluctance. "Ramu, it seems that Anika is getting a little closer to Raj."

"Well, that's natural. The two hang out together almost every day."

"I know," the mother concedes. "They seem to have developed a daily routine. They take morning jogs, then breakfast together. Then there are lunch outings, and then out on the town in the evenings. It's almost as if they were childhood friends."

"Friendship is the foundation of any lasting relationship."

Meena now looks concerned. "That's my fear. Ramu, do you think they're getting too close to each other?"

"I get the feeling they simply enjoy each other's company. Nothing wrong with that. Madam, you know as well as I do, Anika has a tough time finding companionship outside of this home. It's healthy for her to have someone that she can talk to and relate to that's not her mother or her father."

"I understand. It's just that..."

"Just what?" he peers into Meena's concerned eyes.

She pauses for a few seconds before responding. "It's just that... I don't know. I'm just a worried mother, that's all."

"Anything of concern, madam?"

"For example, just yesterday, I noticed that Anika stopped calling him 'Uncle Raj,' she now calls him just 'Raj.' I mentioned this to Anika, and she tells me that Raj doesn't like being called 'Uncle.' "

"Maybe it's true."

"That's absurd. I've never noticed that."

"You must be right then," Ramu says, trying to placate Meena.

The mother continues, "Anika's such a bright girl. She used to visit the orphanage all the time. But since my daughter graduated from school, things have changed. Now she wants to 'redefine and refine her outlook on life.' But instead, she spends all her free time just hanging around."

"Madam, have you tried bringing this up with Prakash?"

"Prakash is so busy with work. He has no idea what's going on, but I see and observe everything. I just want my daughter to start a career and lead a productive life."

"I know you want the best for your daughter. But I don't think it's a bad thing that she's found somebody that she can confide in. She has found someone that she feels comfortable around. Somebody that enjoys similar tastes in life. And most of all, Raj respects her like an equal."

Meena is not able to comprehend any of this. "Even so, why can't she just call him 'Uncle Raj'? Would that be so hard?"

"Life's not supposed to be easy, I guess."

The mother breathes a sigh of resignation. "I guess you're right, Ramu."

The Golden Ganesh

On the other side of Mumbai, Rustom and Billu are taking a walk along Juhu Beach. The beach connects the city to the Arabian Sea and is often less busy this time of day. A few scattered crowds enjoy the refreshing ocean water or walk along the almost empty shore.

A small group of old women practice yoga on the sand. They are diligent in following the lead of their instructor. The leader is an even older woman, but she is fit and in incredible shape. It is a hot day, and there are no clouds in the sky. The air is thick and heavy.

The father and son walk towards a coconut water stand, parked near the road. From a distance, as they approach, Rustom signals the proprietor. The father puts up two fingers, suggesting his order.

The proprietor is a slim, middle-aged man with a blue baseball cap (New York Yankees). He wears a dusty old plaid shirt and ripped jean shorts. His weathered skin is as dirty as his shirt. When he smiles, a significant gap shows at the top of his mouth. But he never smiles, and hardly ever speaks for this reason. The vendor nods back and begins to prepare two coconuts from his big pile.

The small mountain of coconuts rests on top of a large cart. The man pulls the wooden trolley to this street corner each day from the centre of the city, where he sleeps at night. Half of the cart contains his merchandise. The other half contains his household items. The vehicle is all that he has. It is his home, his business, his transportation, and his warehouse all at the same time.

Each coconut takes less than a minute to prepare. The vendor first takes his machete and chops around the sides and then across the top. This reveals the liquid inside from a hole that is as round as a large coin. He then takes the coconut top and carves a small spoon to scoop out the meat from the inside. The vendor rests the spoon together with a straw in the opening. He then hands Rustom the first coconut and then begins to prepare the second one.

Rustom and Billu then move towards the side of the cart to enjoy their refreshing drinks. About this time, a well-dressed, short but also lanky woman approaches the stand. She is wearing a lavish sari, and she adorns a considerable amount of gaudy jewellery. A golden *Ganesh*, the size of a toddler's fist, rests on her chest. It hangs from a thick chain that attempts to weigh down her sari should her garment attempt to escape.

"How much for one coconut drink?" the woman inquires.

The proprietor points to a sign on the cart, which reads, "Forty-five rupees. No tax extra."

"You are a mad man!" the woman screams.

Rustom and Billu overhear this and turn their attention towards the stand. The father is afraid that somebody had a heart attack.

"Madam," the proprietor responds at a slow and even pace, "that's the price. If you cannot afford the price, then I'm sorry."

Rustom is at first concerned but then notices that nobody is in danger. "Lady, what seems to be the problem?" he inquires.

The woman yells back, still angry, and now insulted. "This man. He's trying to rip me off."

"Did he try to steal your money?" the father asks.

"No. But the guy at the train station only charges me forty rupees for one coconut water drink. This guy is asking for forty-five rupees."

Upon hearing this, Rustom looks towards the vendor, who shrugs his shoulders. The father then turns his attention towards the woman and begins to scold her. "Lady, do you also shout when you visit your jeweller when you don't get the price you want?"

She is somewhat confused and taken back by Rustom's question. "No, why would I?"

"Then why are you yelling here? If you want to pay forty rupees for a coconut drink, then go to the train station."

The woman responds (oblivious to the irony of her response), "But I don't want to walk that far, and this is the only coconut stand around. I should not have to pay more just because we're not at the train station."

"Yes, but it's not his fault that you're too lazy to walk that far," Rustom fires back.

"Why don't you mind your own business?" She turns towards the proprietor. "I'm giving you zero stars on Yelp!"

The vendor seems undisturbed, and he gives another shrug. The woman then turns around and walks away, fuming.

Rustom turns towards his son. "Can you believe it? Haggling over five rupees to a vendor trying to make a living for his family. I bet that woman doesn't even attempt to bargain whenever she visits her jeweller. What is society coming to?"

Billu gives a shrug while still sipping his drink.

The Duchess

It is a relaxing Sunday evening at the Malhotra household. Prakash is not on call, so he is home early. He and Raj sit in the backyard at a table near the garden that is between the pool house and the main house. The table is square and painted white, but the chairs are wooden and for the most part, comfortable.

Prakash is having chai, a spicy herbal milk-tea. And with it, he is enjoying *jalebi* and *gathiya*. Ramla made the batch recently, so the *jalebi* is fresh and piping hot. The ingredients are simple. Deep-fried flour sprinkled with saffron. And then drenched in a sugary syrup. It is perfect with *gathiya*, which is a savoury blend of chickpea flour and spices; also deep-fried, but not crunchy. It would seem the phrase 'sugar and spice' was created for this specific combination. For Prakash, he considers this treat along with his chai to be his 'Sunday Heaven.'

Raj sips on ice water and munches on beans and nuts from a bowl in front of himself.

A cool mist from the fountain fills the air as a warm breeze passes through the city. It is cloudy and comfortable outside. And the sun is on its way home, almost out of sight.

"Old friend," the father begins, "what have you been doing with yourself all these years in Goa?"

"Where has the time gone?" Raj shrugs his shoulders. "Just keeping busy, I guess," he surmises.

"And how come you never settled down? Started a family?" Prakash interrogates, like a father to a son.

"It wasn't my fate, I guess. Perhaps..." Raj pauses for a second.

Before the guest can finish replying, Prakash steers the conversation in another direction. "You should have pursued a career in medicine. You could have become a successful doctor, like me, and be making over two crore a year. It's a good life, Raj." Prakash leans back in his chair and spreads his arms wide as if to further highlight the grandeur of his life's work. "It's a comfortable life."

"That's great, but I actually pay more in taxes each quarter," Raj responds with a hearty, but happy laugh.

The doctor laughs at his friend's joke. "Stop kidding around and take life seriously, Raj. You only get one chance to make your mark on the world."

Raj understands that his friend does not believe him. Yet, this does not concern Raj in the slightest. "Prakash, I understand where you're coming from, but success is relative."

"But you're too smart, Raj. At school, you knew more about biology, chemistry, and medicine than almost any student. It's such a shame to not put that potential to work."

"I'm happy with where I am in life, old friend," the guest counters. "I believe in simplicity and in peace. This is great." He leans back in his chair and spreads his arms wide, emulating Prakash from a few moments ago. "For me, simplicity and peace are the most important things in my life."

Unable to consider Raj's perspective, Prakash feels frustrated. The doctor wants Raj to understand that he is only looking out for his friend's well-being. He wants Raj to accept his worldview. But the friend does not value what Prakash values, and vice-versa. This much is clear to Raj, at least.

"I hope you know what you're doing. I worry for you, that's all," Prakash says out loud, but more to himself.

"I assure you, old man, no matter what happens, I will be okay."

This does little to convince the patriarch. But he drops the line of questioning. At this point, Anika and Meena come out of the house and walk towards where the men are sitting.

"Ah, here come my two most beautiful ladies," Prakash says. "Come. Have a seat."

The mother is carrying a tray of snacks, which she places on the table. The young lady has a second tray, which she places next to her mother's. Anika takes a seat opposite Raj, and Meena takes one opposite her husband.

Prakash reaches towards one of the bowls on Anika's tray and places a *mithai* on his plate. He takes a bite and then looks at his wife. "Meena, did you know that Raj makes more than all of the doctors on our block, combined?"

"Well, I've seen his shoes," the wife replies, "so I'm sure that must be the case." She gives the guest a wink.

They all look down at Raj's feet and give a laugh, as they all notice that one of Raj's shoes has a hole in it. Raj replies with a smile. "They're more sentimental to me than anything."

They all laugh again, except for Anika, who has a more nuanced understanding of Raj's humour. Then, switching the subject, the daughter inquires trying to make small talk, "So, are you a big cricket fan?"

"In truth, no," Raj replies. "I've never seen a game, but I would love to one day."

The father considers this unimaginable. "What? I don't believe you."

The guest looks at his friend in the eye. "There are only so many hours in a day... right, my friend?" He then gives Prakash a wink.

At this point, Anika's phone rings, which she had placed between the first and second tray on the table. Without hesitation, Raj reaches for the phone and answers it. He then sets the phone to his ear. "Hello, this is Anika Enterprises. How can we help you today?"

The woman on the other end of the phone answers. "Hello, my good name is Neha from New Fashion Stores. Can I please speak to Ms. Anika?"

"Oh yeah, what's your bad name?" Raj replies.

"Excuse me, sir? May I please speak to Ms. Anika?"

"Sure thing. The duchess just finished having tea with the Queen. You may speak to her now, but you only have thirty seconds. Ready. Set... Go."

Raj passes the phone to Anika, who smiles, takes the phone, and places the phone to her ear. "Hello."

Neha is speaking so fast that her voice squeaks, as she knows that her thirty seconds are almost up. "I'm sorry to interrupt your tea with the Queen, but I have some critical information for you. Information that I think you will want to know."

Anika is now concerned. "Okay, what's the problem?"

"It's about your dress, madam. We have a problem with your dress."

The young lady is now more concerned. "What's wrong with my dress?"

"The designer will no longer be able to make your dress."

Anika's demeanour changes in an instant, and she now feels dismayed. "Why not? What's the problem? I already paid my deposit for the dress and everything."

"Madam, it's already been thirty seconds, should I continue?"

Anika begins to get agitated. "Yes, of course, please continue," she insists.

"It seems that the dress is coming out smaller than the designer expected."

"So why not make it bigger? This sounds like rubbish to me."

"Please be polite, madam. This call is being recorded for training purposes."

The young lady feels exasperated. "Okay, so now what do I do?"

"I see that you have paid a deposit of five thousand rupees for the dress. We will be happy to refund you four thousand and five hundred rupees for your trouble."

Anika is incredulous at this point. "This must be a joke."

"Duchess, I assure you. I would never joke with a friend of the Queen."

"But why can't you refund me the full five thousand?"

Neha responds in a matter-of-fact tone. "It's our policy to deduct five hundred rupees for all cancellations. It's our call centre charge for chai. Have you ever seen the movie, *Slumdog Millionaire*?"

Before Anika can respond, Neha continues. "Don't worry, we'll place a credit to your credit card over the next sixty to one hundred eighty days."

Anika gives a sigh of resignation and hangs up the phone. "Incredible," she says out loud to the table.

The young lady puts the phone down and looks across the table. Raj responds, half-laughing, "Well, that's terrible. I was just warming up to Neha. I was going to ask for her number, maybe take her on a date."

"Listen, body!" Anika scolds, as she points a finger into Raj's face.

"It's 'buddy,' not 'body,'" Raj muses.

"Humph, whatever," grumbles the young lady.

The mother and father look back and forth between Raj and Anika, and they begin to laugh out loud.

"Don't you worry," Anika replies, "we're still going to this party in style. We'll just have to get a readymade dress from the mall."

"What do you mean by 'we'll,' young lady?" Raj questions.

Anika looks into Raj's eyes with a stern expression on her face. "Yes, I insist you come with me."

"It's okay," Raj counters. "I don't need anything from the mall."

"I'm talking about the party. I need someone to accompany me. Do you want me to go all by myself?"

Meena steps in. "Anika, I don't think Uncle Raj would like to go to some random kid's party."

The daughter now turns towards her mother. "Mommy, he's not some random kid. He's Uncle Bhat's son. We went to the same grade school. I used to play volleyball with his sister, Vihaan. Do you remember her? She's the one who always asked for rides home from practice? Her mother always worked late most evenings."

Prakash now chimes in. "Oh, Meena! She has a good point; you don't want Anika to go to the party by herself, do you? Plus, it's just one evening. Ramu will take them and bring them back safely."

Anika is swift to stand up now that she has her father's consent. "Great, it's settled. Get ready, mister, we're going to the mall."

Raj is unable to say 'no' and so he bellows, "As you wish."

The Bass

It is the evening of the graduation, and Ramu, driving the family car, pulls up to a big house at the top of a hill. Raj and Anika sit in the back seat in comfortable silence. Both seem placid, but also sleepy. It is quarter past seven, and the night is young, or at least that is what they tell themselves.

Once the car comes to a stop, the driver places the vehicle in park, and he proceeds to open his door. In an instant, clubbing music with heavy bass radiates from the house. Vivacious, young voices cheering, and yelling pour out from the packed structure. Raj and Anika look at each other and take a long sigh. It seems the evening will need more energy than they have right now.

"I'm getting too old for this," Anika whispers to herself.

"You're telling me?" Raj whispers back.

Before stepping out of the car, Ramu turns towards the couple in the back seat. "Okay, kids, I'll go meet some friends in town. Ring me when you're ready to go home."

"Yes, Ramu," they reply in unison.

"And don't forget to have fun," the chauffeur continues.

"Yes, Ramu," they reply in unison.

"And don't drink too much," he continues.

"Yes, Ramu," they reply in unison, one last time.

The Stars and the Moon

The party is grand. The music is loud. The house is full of youth enjoying themselves. The interior of the house is elegant but modern and minimal. It could be that most of the furniture had already been moved aside. What is visible seems to be enough to accommodate a small family without young children.

An overpopulated dance floor consumes the living room from within. A DJ spins records in the corner. The air radiates with heat from all dancers. Everyone seems full of energy and vigour. Libations are flowing without constraint.

Near the far end of the living room is a big sliding glass door that connects to the deck that overlooks the city. Most of the partygoers are younger than Anika, and at first, Raj feels out of place.

Anika picks up on this. So she grabs Raj by the hand and leads him through the living room dance floor towards the bar on the deck. "How about we get you a KF?" the young lady yells back at him.

Raj smiles and gives her the thumbs up with his free hand.

As they meander through the crowd, some of the partygoers take notice of the couple. Some make curious faces. But most pay no attention.

The young lady steps up to the bar, and Raj stands a few feet back. The bartender is a young male with a black t-shirt, jeans, and a yellow and purple Hawaiian leu around his neck.

Anika leans forward so the bartender can hear her order. "I'll have one KF and one Sprite, please."

The bartender pours the drinks into plastic, red Solo cups and hands the cups to Anika. The young lady passes the cup with beer to Raj, and they step towards the edge of the deck, facing the city.

The stars are out, and the full moon is shining overhead with minimal clouds blocking the way.

"Cheers to the stars and the moon." She taps her plastic cup against Raj's.

"Cheers," he smiles back.

They take a brief but noticeable glance into each other's eyes. They smile at the same time. And then they take their sips as they look up into the heavens. The couple spends the next few minutes taking in the grand view. The fresh air high on this hill gives them a bit of energy, but also some comfort. They feel solitude, and content and warm.

"Do you like this music?" Raj asks after a while.

"Never heard of it. I'm more into classic rock."

"How do you dance to classic rock, though?" Raj inquires.

"Not sure; let's find out," Anika responds, and they head towards the DJ by the dance floor, and the young lady whispers a suggestion into the DJ's ear, who nods back in agreement.

Soon after, the tempo picks up. The crowd is raving, and the party becomes even livelier. Raj and Anika proceed to dance the night away. To the young lady, Raj seems to be able to adapt to new environments as if he can transform identities at will.

Anika wishes this quality for herself sometimes. So from this perspective, she feels envy towards Raj's ability to adapt. The young lady yearns to experience new and exciting things all the time. But she often is reluctant to chase her desires. Something always seems to hold her back. Most of the time, it is the feeling that she should be doing something different. Something grander. Something more meaningful. This is why at first, she was reluctant about attending this evening's festivities. But now that Anika is here, and now that Raj is with her, all her insecurities seemed to have melted away. At least for the moment.

At the same time, the young lady feels intrigued by Raj. And the mystery of this man is beginning to take hold of her subconscious. Yet she does her best to not fester on such thoughts. But also, it has been a few weeks since they met, and Anika has noticed other peculiarities over this time. Like Raj always seems to need to run off every now and then. Granted, when he returns, it is as if he never left. He did this twice this evening. But each time, he came back energized and charged up.

A part of Anika tells herself there must be something deeper going on with the man. Her brain registers concern. Concern that he may be dealing with something or someone troubling. But another part of her concedes that this is none of her business. Raj is a grown man after all, and he has his own life to deal with.

Even into the late hours, Raj keeps up with the youngsters without issue. Anika feels impressed with not only his stamina but also his dancing style. She did not expect Raj to be so comfortable on the dance floor. But at this point, the young lady is not so surprised either. "An evening to remember," Anika thinks to herself at one point.

The Arcade

Towards the end of the night, Anika and Raj head back out to the balcony for some fresh air. The young lady confesses, although she is still out of breath, "Wow, mister, I'm quite impressed."

"Impressed? By what?"

"I didn't think you would be such a good dancer," she exclaims.

"Did you think people started dancing only after you were born?" Raj questions.

"It's not that. It's just that I imagined that people danced differently back in the day."

"What? Like this?" Raj begins to dance like a robot.

"That's too good," Anika responds with a laugh. "But not quite what I meant."

They both lean on the railing of the deck and look out towards the city. For a moment, they pause to take in the view and the fullness of the night. Yet, Raj, being responsible, maintains his composure, and he keeps his distance. The couple each want to say something about how they feel a growing connection, but both are unsure how to go about saying such a thing. Even so, there is a noticeable increase in the amount of eye contact between the two.

"Raj, I want to thank you for a good time tonight," the young lady begins.

"You're welcome," Raj responds.

"Can I ask you something?"

"Sure, you can ask me anything."

"It's personal—I don't want to upset you." The young lady begins to feel reluctant.

"Don't worry. Just because you ask doesn't mean I have to answer. So go ahead, ask away," Raj affirms.

"Good point, but sometimes I worry that I offend others with my questions. That's all."

"Yeah, but that's not your problem; that's their problem. As long as you ask with good intentions, it shouldn't bother you if others get offended," Raj counters.

"I guess that makes sense." Anika pauses for a second and then continues. "I'm just wondering... how come you never got married, Raj?"

"How do you know I'm not married?" Raj replies with a smile.

Anika had never considered this. All this time, the young lady assumed that Raj was not married. In fact, she did not even think the man could be in a relationship. He had never mentioned anyone. But then again, she had never asked or inquired up until this point. Upon hearing this, the young lady's mind shifts to an uncomfortable place. She is not sure why, either. But this only lasts for a moment. After a pause, Anika continues. "Well, you don't have a ring, and you've never mentioned anyone," she replies, in a soft voice so as not to offend her guest.

Raj is still leaning over the railing. His fingers rest crossed before himself, and he is looking up at the heavens.

His eyes are following the path of an airplane, crossing the sky in the distance. There is an infinite twinkle of lights in the distance. It is past midnight, and the city is alive. And the sounds of countless lives hustling and bustling about radiate from the metropolis far below.

Raj looks to his left, at the young lady to his side, and explains himself, "No cause for alarm. Listen, I'm not in a relationship with anyone if that's what you're wondering about. The reason is simple. A match never came along. And I've just been too busy all these years to do anything about it," he replies, almost with resignation.

Anika takes in his response but has a sceptical look on her face. "I find it very hard to believe that after all these years, you've never found someone."

"Well, there was someone," Raj responds after a pause. "But it didn't end well."

"Oh my! What happened?" Anika inquires, fearing the worst.

"Just before the engagement, I went out with the girl on a date. We went for pizza, not too far from the jetty where I used to play as a kid. I was sitting there, enjoying my slice, right across from this young lady. And suddenly, it dawned on me."

"What was that?" Anika's mind fills with intrigue.

"That she couldn't smile."

"What do you mean, she couldn't smile? Everyone can smile!" Anika can hardly control her own smile while saying this.

"Nope. Not this woman. I thought back to myself that I had never once seen her smile. Sitting across from her, I then tried to smile myself, hoping to get a reaction. I tried jokes. I even tried getting her an ice cream sundae after the pizza. Nothing worked. She couldn't smile."

"I don't believe you, Raj," Anika responds with a hearty laugh.

"No, I'm serious. I ended it that very night. How could I spend the rest of my life with someone who can't smile? I am convinced that the personality of a woman is reflected in her smile. Personality doesn't come from makeup or fancy clothes. It comes from one's smile. And this woman simply couldn't smile. So, I called off the whole thing that very night." He ends with a grin.

Anika can't keep from laughing, and she rests her hand on his shoulder, almost for support. "Okay, Raj, I know there's more to this than you're letting on. But I'll end the interrogation. For now."

"My life is an open book, I assure you, Anika," he concludes. Then after a pause, he asks her a question, "So, how about you? Anyone special in your life?"

Anika goes silent. She then speaks out while still leaning over the railing, her tummy resting on the ledge. Anika looks into the depths of the city. And she confesses to the night sky, "I guess I have my own commitment issues."

"Maybe you prefer to have options?"

The young lady stares down at her hands for solace. And then she crosses her arms in front of herself, and she begins to scratch her elbows. "I guess you can call it that.

But really, I can't seem to find anything or anyone that I can stick to. Something always happens."

"Like when you stopped going to the orphanage?"

"Yes, like the orphan... wait, how did you know?" Not even her parents know that Anika stopped going. And she hasn't mentioned the orphanage for some time, so she feels shocked to hear that Raj knows that she was fired.

"I just know." Raj gives a stoic reply. Raj recalled from their dinner last week that Anika mentioned that she hasn't been going lately. And since he has been a guest of the family, the young lady has not volunteered there once. Also, Raj sensed a general reluctance in Anika to discuss the topic. Given all this, Raj assumed something must have happened.

"It's a long story. And I don't want to trouble you with it." The young woman's demeanour becomes meek.

"Don't worry. I have all night." Raj opens his arms wide as if to show that the night is still young. He then turns to face her. "Listen, Anika, you don't have to tell me if you don't want to. But I'm here to listen if you need me."

Anika has been reluctant to tell anyone about what happened last month. She even tries to hide the truth from herself. But all this does is further contribute to her anxiety and insomnia. The young lady takes a deep breath, and then she lets the hot air out from her lungs, real slow. "Okay, here it goes. So, I was taking care of the pre-schoolers and pre-teens all by myself. And I decided to give the kids a treat and take them to a movie. On the way, one of the boys went missing."

"What did you do?"

"I immediately went back to the orphanage to tell Gaurav." The young lady's voice begins to quiver as she starts to get more tense and emotional.

"Wait, who's Gaurav?"

"He's the manager. He thinks he runs the place. But really, the volunteers do all the work. He's just been there so long that he thinks he knows everything. But Gaurav didn't even let me explain myself. All he did is yell. Can you believe it?"

"So, what happened to the boy?"

"We found him at the arcade later that day."

"That's crazy."

"Gaurav blamed me for everything, saying it was all my fault. He fired me that day, and I haven't been back since. I was good at my job too. Or at least, I thought I was."

"I see."

"Wait, so you're taking Gaurav's side on this?"

"No, I didn't say that."

"Well, what do you say now? That I'm a failure, right?" The young lady's face becomes red, and she feels uncontrollable angst as her heart begins to race.

"Question. Did you try your best that day?" Raj asks with a calm expression in his voice.

"Of course, I did."

"Then you have nothing to worry about."

"But you don't get it. I lost my job. I know it was unpaid, but still." Anika feels hysterical as her emotions are fully charged now.

"That's Gaurav's loss, not yours. There are thousands of places to volunteer in this city."

"I guess, but I still feel like a failure. It was my fault that the kid went missing, after all."

"First things first. There's nothing wrong with failure. You cannot succeed without failure. Second, that incident doesn't sound like it was your fault. After all, you tried your best. Third, even though it wasn't your fault, it was your responsibility. There's an enormous difference between fault and responsibility."

"I'm not following." Her voice begins to soften.

"I've learned a few things having to take charge over the years. But the most important thing I have picked up is that bad stuff will happen no matter how good your intentions are. Even so, it is the responsibility of those in charge to take control when trouble arrives. Not because they are to blame, but because they have the power to act. You see? It's not about fault, it's about responsibility. Does that make sense?" Raj stays silent while the young lady digests this.

"Perhaps. I think so." Anika whispers.

"That's the difference between a manager, like your boss. Someone who only believes in blame and punishment. And a leader like Gandhi, who believed in making the world better, but with compassion and fairness."

"Sounds so easy when you say it like that."

"In fact, it's quite the opposite. It's hard. Indeed, life is not supposed to be easy. But as Mahatma once said, 'If you worry about yesterday's failures, then today's successes will be few. Your future depends on what you do today.'"

Anika is now silent. This is a significant amount of information to take in so late in the evening. So her brain records the conversation, which she will unwrap at her own pace. But inside, deep in her heart, she feels cathartic. It is as if she can finally take a full breath of fresh air after sinking in quicksand for so long. And so she does. The young lady breaths in and lets it out at a slow, metered pace. Goosebumps ride up her arms, and her body gives a slight shiver. "Thank you, Raj. I feel better. But I might need to have you explain all this to me again tomorrow."

"I'd love to, but I'm busy."

"Oh yeah?" The young lady frowns.

"I have a date with Gaurav tomorrow. We're playing PacMan at the arcade." Raj manages to keep a placid expression on his face while saying this.

Anika places her hands on her hips, fists closed, and gives Raj a smile. "Listen, body."

Raj replies, smiling, "It's not 'body,' it's 'buddy.'"

The young lady begins to retort, but before she can respond, Raj continues. "You're right, though." After pausing for a moment, he continues. "'Listen, body' does mean something, in fact."

Anika is silent now but looks back at Raj, with confusion in her eyes, and Raj begins again. "After someone dies, that person's name goes away, and the person is instead just referred to as a body."

She wears a sceptical expression across her face, but the young lady is curious to see where Raj is going with this. "During a funeral, they always say, 'the body is going to leave for cremation in the morning' he begins.

"Right, so..." Anika tries to follow, but her brain is beginning to slow down.

Raj continues, "Or they say, 'the final rites are being performed on the body,' or 'while the body is cremated, the ashes will be dispersed in the holy river.' You see, it's always about the body. And one day your buddy will be a body, too."

Anika whispers, "I see."

"I don't think we magically turn into bodies after we die. We're bodies when we're alive as well. It's just that when we're alive, we get to smile more. So, from this perspective, I think 'listen, body' is just as good as 'listen, buddy.'"

The young lady is appreciative of Raj's thoughtful comments. "Interesting philosophy, I must say."

Raj allows himself to consider for the first time if he really has feelings for the young lady next to him. It is at this point where he considers Anika to be more like an equal than anything. But also, he considers her to be a true friend and companion, which is something that has been missing in his life for so long. "I know she's younger than me, but age is just a number. What matters most is mutual respect," he considers to himself as he stares into Anika's dark glimmering eyes.

The two gaze into each other's eyes with a shared but unspoken understanding. And after a moment's pause, they turn towards the city and look up into the sky once again.

The Window

It is late night, and the family automobile pulls into the driveway back at home. Ramu drives, and Raj is next to him in the front seat. And Anika lies in the back, sleeping, with her head up against the window. Her shoes are off. And her feet extend on the seat below her body.

As the car pulls to a stop, Meena is visible from the window of her room, which overlooks the front courtyard. The mother has been awaiting her daughter's return. She has an anxious look on her face. Prakash is not around. But he is likely working late, given that he is on-call with the hospital this evening.

Meena observes Raj exiting the vehicle, and she sees him open the car door for Anika. Raj taps Anika awake with a gentleness that Meena did not expect. The daughter wakes up and gives the man a smile (though she is still half-asleep). He then extends his hand inside the car, and Anika allows herself to be lifted out of the vehicle.

"Can you make it to your room without getting lost?" Raj asks.

Anika replies (half-asleep, and with one eye open), "I'm fine, thank you. Don't worry about me. I'll manage to get back."

"Okay then, goodnight."

Anika yawns as she begins to slink back towards the house at a slow and uneven pace. "Night. No running tomorrow. Will sleep in."

Raj responds with a nod and a smile, which Anika cannot see, but Meena takes notice. Raj then turns and begins to walk back towards the pool house.

Throughout this interaction, the mother's expression goes through a metamorphosis. At first, she feels fear and trepidation. Of course, she often worries about her daughter. But this time is different. This time the mother feels dread. Yet, seeing Anika return safely in the hands of their house guest causes a profound change in the mother's heart.

Now, Meena picks up on something that she was not expecting. She noticed a pure sincerity in the encounter that she had witnessed. The mother felt a warm sincerity between Raj and her daughter. In particular, she takes note of deep respect and an innocent affection between the two. Not as with a romantic couple, but more so as with a companionship built upon a mutual understanding.

This gives the matriarch pause. But the mother has no idea what to do with these new feelings. For the time being, she lets out a big sigh as she backs away from the window.

The Milk

A few minutes later, Anika stumbles into the kitchen. The young lady manages to open the refrigerator door with effort and a few missteps. But now, she sticks her head and shoulders inside the refrigerator and stops motionless. She stands there, without moving for a while.

Meena enters the kitchen. "You don't plan on sleeping in there, dear, do you?"

Anika responds, but she is half-asleep and half lost in thought, "No, Mommy."

"Did you have a fun night?" the mother inquires.

"Yes, Mommy."

"What did you do?"

"Nothing. We ate a bunch."

"Oh yeah? What did you eat?"

Anika grabs the jug of milk and closes the door to the fridge.

"Snacks. You know, party snacks."

"You were gone all night, and all you did was eat a bunch of snacks?"

Anika puts the jug down, pours herself a glass, and finishes it one big gulp. "Mommy, I'm exhausted."

Meena capitulates. "Okay, dear. Get some rest."

The mother then steps up to Anika and gives her daughter a hug. The young lady puts the glass down and turns towards her mom. Anika returns the hug, but she wears an expression of listlessness and exhaustion.

Meena leans back and places both of her hands on her daughter's shoulders and looks into her eyes. "You know, I love you very much."

Anika tries to fake a smile but exhaustion tugs at her entire body. "I love you too, Mommy."

"I only want the best for you, dear."

"I know, Mommy. It's just that I've had a long day, and I'm very sleepy now."

"Okay, get some rest, dear."

Anika proceeds to make her way back towards her room with one eye closed. She keeps both arms stretched out in front of her so as not to bump into anything while on her journey.

Meena returns to bed. The mother did not fall asleep for some time, as her thoughts continued to race. But still, she laid down more secure in her being than earlier that night. The feeling of dread was less than before. Now her usual worry had returned. Yet she finally drifted off to sleep just as the sun returned to work for the day.

The Swallows

The morning after the graduation party, Raj has an important decision to make. Either hang out here in Mumbai until the end of the week or go back to Goa before it is too late. Something tells him that going back home would be best. After all, the man's life is in Goa. Ram Iqbal, his half-brother, is keeping an eye on his affairs. But at the same time, Raj had never taken a break this long in twenty-five years. And because of this, Raj is anxious to return.

After laying in his bed for some time, Raj stands up. He looks at his belongings and he considers whether to pack his backpack to leave. It would not take him too long because he had brought so little with him. Not sure how to proceed, Raj makes his way out of the pool house for fresh air.

It is early in the dawn, and the swallows begin to wake. They chirp and tweet from all directions as if they are trying to interrogate Raj. Raj passes around the side of the house with care as he does not want to disturb the sleeping house. He takes slow steps to avoid confrontation from his feathered and non-feathered friends.

Raj then pauses in the front driveway, near the fountain. The man does not have a specific plan, but for now, he thinks he should return home yet his heart is conflicted.

And as he is standing there, Raj takes a few moments to take in the morning air. All the birds are awake at this point, and the city outside is coming to life. The fountain is jubilant and dancing; it has already had its morning coffee, it seems to Raj. The freshness of the scene makes Raj realize that it has been a long time since he has felt this alive.

Sometimes we go through life, and we forget. We forget that there are entirely different experiences out there. Situations and events that we would never encounter in our day-to-day lives. And because we do not notice any of this, we go about our business as if these alternate realities do not even exist.

Now Raj feels more awake then he has in a long time. He looks up at the grand house and considers all the fond memories enclosed within its sturdy walls. The birth of a child, the first big party, the family dinners. Despite these lingering thoughts, Raj still thinks he should get back to his home. He takes out his phone and thinks about calling an Uber. But first, he calls Ram Iqbal to inform him of his intended arrival.

Yet, Ram Iqbal implores Raj to not return. As if he is not wanted, it seems to Raj. "We need to be able to run things without you, brother." Ram Iqbal pleads. And then, "If you get hit by a bus, the business must go on. We need the practice of your absence. Trust me."

"Great. Now what? I should have just called him once I was on the train," Raj thinks to himself.

But in truth, Ram Iqbal wanted his brother to take a long break from his hectic life. The brother had noticed that Raj was becoming too engrossed in his work affairs. Before Raj left for Mumbai, he had not slept for three days working on a last-minute business deal. But there were always deals to make. And there was always business to do. Even so, Raj knew he was burning out. Yet, he never mentioned it to anyone, even to Ram Iqbal. But his brother knew better.

"Okay, brother. I'll give you until the end of the week." Raj hangs up the phone, and he lets out a deep sigh.

The Big File

Over the next few days, Prakash does his best to convince Raj to stay longer.

"Don't tell me you have something more important going on in your life right now."

"Mumbai grows on you like a vine. Once the city takes you in, there's no escape."

"You'll come for the people and experience, but you'll stay for life."

Prakash can go on and on about his beloved city.

"Plus, I need some help with a project. You keep saying you're in business. Well, a businessman is exactly what I need," the father admits that Friday over breakfast. "Follow me into my office," Prakash leads the way.

Raj finishes his ice water and follows the man. He is covered in sweat, but the cold liquid helps to cool him down. Raj has finished his morning jog, but he still needs to rehydrate more as he wipes off his brow with the back of his hand.

Inside the office, Prakash takes out a big file and begins to go through it with Raj. "I want to build the biggest temple Mumbai has ever seen."

Over the next half-hour, the father relates to his friend his dream. "It will be grand. It will be hand-carved, out of marble. People from all over will come to marvel at its grandeur."

"Have you ever done anything like this before?" Raj looks puzzled after trying to digest his friend's plans.

"Where there is a will, there is a way. Isn't your middle name, 'Will'?" Prakash gives Raj a wink.

The friend is quick to realize that Prakash is way over his head. The rough plan that the doctor has so far shared leads Raj to believe that the project will likely end up as a disaster. It will probably end up costing twice as much. And it will take twice as long to build. And it will need twice the amount of people to get it done. But this is only with an incredible amount of luck, Raj thinks to himself.

"You know if you don't have perfect execution, this project could ruin you. You're putting your entire financial future behind this one project," Raj explains. He tries his best to share his concerns with Prakash without sounding insulting.

But the doctor is unwavering, "Every man lives, but not every man leaves a legacy. This will be mine. And there's no stopping me."

So with reluctance, Raj agrees to stay on a bit longer to help his friend.

"But don't tell Meena or Anika. I want this to be a big surprise," Prakash closes the big file. He sits back in his sturdy leather chair with a broad smile across his face.

All Raj can do for the moment is to scratch his head in disbelief.

The Valet

Over the next few weeks, Raj develops a stable, comfortable routine. He remains a guest of the Malhotra residence, and he begins to become ever more entwined in their lives. Over this time, Raj does his best to bring Prakash's vision to more stable ground.

One morning, Raj is working through his notes on Prakash's temple project at the nearby Madras Leaf Café. The café makes a decent office. Here, Raj can make progress on his friend's secret project without the rest of the family finding out.

Today, he is enjoying an early morning *dosa* and a Madras coffee. Raj puts down his coffee, picks up the phone, and dials. "Ram Iqbal, fill me in."

The brother responds on the other end. "No news, Raj. Same as yesterday. No need to worry. Everything is under control."

Raj replies (almost sounding disappointed), "Okay, just checking." He puts the phone down, and he turns his attention back to his files. "What a mess this could have been," he thinks to himself.

But at least Raj has made good progress with Prakash's expectations. "The temple does not have to be the biggest temple in Mumbai for it to be the best," Raj explains. He was able to convince his friend to reduce the size, which should make a big difference in the final cost. One small win at a time, it seems to Raj.

The manager walks up to Raj's table and hands him the bill. "Here you go, Raj." The manager is Dhansukh, the same waiter from the eight-star restaurant from a few weeks ago.

"Thank you, Dhansukh," Raj replies.

"Have a good one." The manager nods and steps away.

A few moments later, Rustom and Billu, the father and son duo, pass in front of Raj. Raj gives them a nod. They pause in front of Raj, at first not recognizing him.

He then says, "Rustom, Billu. How are you both today?"

It is unclear if either father or son recognizes Raj. Rustom seems upset, and Billu is lost in thought. After a pause, the father begins to speak, almost to himself. "Can you believe it? Somebody stole my car. At a party, no less. Can you think of a worse time to have your car stolen?"

"Well sure, I guess," Raj replies. "But that's unconscionable."

Rustom is self-absorbed in his predicament and takes little notice of Raj's response. Even so, the father continues (again, as if he's speaking to himself). "Can you believe it? I arrived at a Parsi party. The parking lot was full of cars, so I handed my keys to a guy wearing a red vest, thinking he was a valet driver."

"Sounds sensible to me," Raj replies.

"Turns out the party didn't even have valet parking. The guy in the red vest sped away with my vehicle. Can you believe it?"

"I guess anything's possible in this city."

Rustom frowns. "I know. But I would have never thought that would be possible in Mumbai. Can you believe it?"

Raj understands that the conversation is going nowhere. So he turns his attention to Billu. "How's business, Billu?"

Billu replies with one word. "Okay." He then proceeds to stand there. The young man has an awkward expression on his face, and he stares at Raj's table in silence.

After a few moments, Raj stands up and picks up his files and his bill. He then waves bye to them both. "Well, glad to hear that everything is on the up and up for you both."

The father responds, "Yes, yes, of course."

The son whispers, "Sure."

Rustom and Billu turn and walk away. Raj steps up to the cashier, where Dhansukh is handing a receipt to the customer ahead of Raj. Raj then pays his bill and collects his change. He then picks up a gift card next to the register, and he turns it over. It is blank on the other side. After a short pause, Raj grabs the pen, resting on the checkout counter, and he scribbles something on the back. Raj then places the gift card in his wallet.

Dhansukh notices and says, "Sir, you know the card is empty? You need to fill it first."

Raj places the wallet back in his pocket and turns to leave. "Yes, I know."

He then gives Dhansukh a wink as he exits the café.

The Club

After leaving the café, Raj heads back to the home. He enters the house to find everyone there, busy with their daily activities and chores.

In the corner of the living room, by the bookshelf, Sughandha engrosses herself in a novel. She is reading *The Stranger* by Albert Camus. She plans to finish it before she gets up from her favourite reading spot. Other characters in the novel consider the protagonist to be withdrawn and taciturn. But to Sughandha, the main character's response to this is resplendent, "I just don't have much to say. So I keep quiet."

Upon finishing this passage, she grins to herself in silence. "I would make a great criminal," the woman thinks to herself. "I have no desire to speak, unlike most everyone. It is silly how most suspects end up incriminating themselves. All because they cannot keep their mouths shut." Sughandha has never committed a crime. And it would be quite tricky to do so because she never interacts with anyone. Yet, she knows well, that she would make a great suspect if she were ever taken into custody. And for some reason, this provides the avid reader with a particular type of comfort. A comfort that nobody else will ever know about, which is something that makes the feeling more special.

Anika is wrapping a present on the kitchen table.

"It's too early for Diwali presents, isn't it?" Raj begins as he takes a seat next to her.

The young lady continues her methodical wrapping without looking up. "No. This is a birthday gift. It's Mangla's fifty-fifth today."

Raj nods his head and then pauses for a second. "I have an idea."

"Oh yeah, what's that?" Anika inquires without looking up.

Raj takes out the gift card from his wallet and slides it across the table. "Gather all the Hi-Fi Club maids and take them out for a treat for Mangla's birthday. Here's a gift card for the Madras Leaf Café. There's five thousand on it."

The Hi-Fi Club was a group of maids from the surrounding neighbourhood. Mangla and her friend, Amala, founded the club over twenty years ago. The large group now meets up each month to organize charitable events for the community. But most of the time, they meet up to exchange gossip relating to their employers. They call themselves the Hi-Fi Club because they consider themselves to be high society maids that embrace the latest trends in fashion, technology, and entertainment. So they are not just ordinary maids, but rather maids en vogue.

This last comment from Raj finally grabs Anika's attention. She puts down the tape in her hands, picks up the gift card, sees '5000' written on the back, and then looks up with a smile. "Wow, Raj. That's very generous of you."

"My pleasure," he tips his invisible hat.

The young lady picks up her phone, and she texts Mangla. "Hey, birthday girl, we have a special treat for you today. Gather the Hi-Fi Club and let's all meet at the Madras Leaf Café today at one p.m."

Anika puts down the phone and smiles back at Raj. He gives her the thumbs up.

The Afternoon Nap

Six other Hi-Fi Club members have arrived at the café along with Anika, Sughandha, and Mangla. Sughandha is about to finish her book from earlier this morning, so she does not even look up as she walks into the restaurant. Everyone sits around a large square table near the entrance.

Over the years, Sughandha has become adept at walking and reading at the same time. Her feet can follow the steps of whoever she is tailing. And she does not need to think about where she walks at this point. Sometimes, she ends up somewhere, and she does not even recall how or when she got there.

Dhansukh is the party's waiter, and he approaches the table. "How are you all today?" He recognizes Anika. "And so glad to be serving you again, my lady."

Anika now recognizes the waiter. "Why, hello. Glad to see that everything is on the up and up for you."

"You bet. Now I'll get some real respect. I'm no longer a mere waiter. I'm a manager now," Dhansukh replies, pointing to his nametag (which does not mention that he is a manager).

"Well, today's a special day for us. We're celebrating Mangla's birthday. Let's start with drinks all around!" The young lady motions to the table.

As time passes, the guests enjoy themselves without bound. After two hours, a menagerie of empty glasses, dishes, bowls, and plates consumes the table.

"Well, ladies," Anika boasts, "Shall we have dessert?"

One lady at the table rubs her belly. "Oh my, we're so full."

Another lady concurs, "I don't think I can eat another bite."

A third states, "Okay, but this is it for me."

Mangla chimes in, "I'll take just one bite from your dish."

"Great," Anika replies, "it's settled then." She motions towards Dhansukh, and as he approaches the table, the young lady gives the order. "Dhansukh, please bring us one round of *gulab jamun*."

The manager looks at the table and is quite surprised that these nine women have been able to empty so many dishes. Even so, the waiter calls back, "Yes, madam. Will that be all?"

Anika pauses for a second and then responds. "Yes, please be sure to heat them up, and serve a scoop of pistachio ice cream on top."

Gulab jamun is a spongy, milky treat, flavoured with cardamom. It consists of flour, butter, and milk, deep-fried to perfection. It is then soaked in rose syrup, and it is best served piping hot, but with ice cream on top.

"Very well, madam. Anything else?"

The young lady pauses for another second and then responds. "And let's have nine special orders of *paan* from the vendor outside."

Paan is the ideal pallet cleanser to top off a heavy Indian meal. Betel leaf, a large green leaf, forms the outside casing. Stuffed inside the shell are areca nut, fennel seeds, anise seeds, coconut, and sesame seeds. It is wrapped like a triangle-shaped gift or a flattened *samosa*. But *paan* is best when it is fresh and made to order.

"Yes, madam. Will that be all?"

Anika pauses for another second and then responds. "That'll be all." She then pulls out the card and hands it to Dhansukh. "And please keep the change."

"Very well, thank you," the manager bows as he steps away.

A few minutes later, Dhansukh returns, and he is fuming. "Madam, I don't know what you're trying to pull here, but this gift card is empty."

"That can't be. Check again. Don't worry, it's on there."

"No, madam, I've checked multiple times. In fact, this card has never been activated. What exactly are you trying to pull here?"

Anika feels mortified, and so is everyone else at the table. The young lady looks around the table; she is so confused that she cannot even think straight.

One lady at the table states, "I have ten rupees."

Another lady chirps, "I only have seven rupees with me."

A third lady gives a grunt, "I didn't even come with my wallet."

Mangla pulls out a hundred rupees from her purse, "Here take this."

Yet it becomes evident that the party has nowhere near enough to pay for the meal. Anika opens her wallet only to find a few hundred rupees. She takes out her cash and hands it to the manager. "Here, take it all. It's all I have."

Dhansukh clenches both hands and presses them against his hips. "Madam, you owe thousands more. You cannot leave until this bill is paid in full."

At this point, everyone at the table becomes terrified.

"Let me speak with the manager," Anika responds.

"I am the manager!" Dhansukh shouts, pointing at his badge, now shaking with anger.

The party looks around at each other in disbelief, not sure how to proceed.

After much hassle, the party works out a deal. All nine guests march into the kitchen and line up in a row. Dhansukh comes back from the janitor's closet with supplies. He walks down the row of patrons, and hands each one an apron and a pair of yellow dishwashing gloves. Even Sughandha must put down her book.

Each member helps to wash the dishes in an assembly line fashion. And from the massive pile of dishes, many of them theirs, it is clear that they will be busy at it for quite some time.

Meanwhile, back at home, Raj is fast asleep in the pool house, enjoying an afternoon nap. Raj has a small but visible smile on his face.

The Last Laugh

It is now later that evening, and the family (except for Anika, but including Raj) is enjoying dinner in the dining room. As usual, Ramla has whipped up a feast. This is a typical meal for the family, but still, there are no less than three separate dishes for the entree alone.

Half-way through the meal, Anika walks in. Her hair is a mess, and she looks dishevelled and exhausted. The young lady walks up to the dinner table and stands in front of Raj. "Hey, mister! Let me know one thing. What in the world were you thinking?"

Raj replies without hesitation, "I'm not sure what you're talking about."

Anika cuts him off. "You know very well. That gift card was empty. You set me up!"

Raj, still calm, retorts with a smile. "I said it has five thousand on it, and that's true. I wrote '5000' on the card."

Anika is not pleased in the slightest. "You knew very well that I would think the card was loaded with rupees."

Prakash gives a big laugh. "Let this be a lesson to you. Remember, young lady, never assume anything." He then points to Raj. "Especially with this one."

Everyone has a big laugh, except for Anika, who is still upset. A small part of her realizes that she was not innocent in the fiasco. After all, she could have double-checked the card first. And she has noticed Raj pull similar pranks before. Yet, the young lady never thought she would be in the centre of one of them. As such, her ego refuses to let Raj off the hook.

Raj continues, "Your father's right. Things are not always what they seem. But don't worry, the fun can't last forever. I must return to the real world soon. I plan to head back to Goa this weekend."

He has all but wrapped up working out the fine details of Prakash's grand temple project. The guest reviewed the final details with the doctor before dinner. To his surprise, the doctor accepted all the crucial changes that Raj had suggested. The guest had also found a trustworthy contractor to take over the initiative in his absence. Given all this, Raj is no longer concerned about the project's future success.

At the same time, Raj received troubling news about his business earlier that day. The deal that he had prepared before he left town fell through. Nothing Ram Iqbal could not handle. But Raj knew he could solve the stalemate without issue if only he were there in person. For this and many reasons, Raj told his half-brother last night that he had already booked a ticket back. "There is no stopping me this time, Ram Iqbal. Plus, I miss your company too much to continue this vacation any longer."

While lying in bed last night, Raj knew going back would not be easy for him. But he also knew that staying in Mumbai too long would cause him to overstay his welcome. He was grateful for having met all these beautiful people. Yet, he knew in his heart, that the party must soon end.

Upon hearing the news at dinner today, everyone becomes subdued. Meena looks in Anika's direction to gauge her reaction. Anika has a blank expression, but she seems unnerved.

Prakash breaks the silence. "We're so glad to have had you, old friend." And he gives him a warm pat on the back.

"It has been a pleasant experience visiting you all," Raj replies. "One that I will never forget. Thank you all for your kind hospitality. I am truly blessed to have been able to stay with you for so long. Do come and visit me anytime. I will miss you all."

Anika's eyes begin to tear up, and her hands are shaking, but she holds her composure. "I hope you keep up with your running. Good habits die young."

Raj gives a thoughtful nod in reply. Meena puts her hand on Anika's side to console her. "Raj, it's been great, and I hope you do visit again." The words almost sound like a whisper as they leave Meena's mouth.

The father, somewhat oblivious to everyone else's reaction, boasts, "Yes, indeed. It's been great. You are always welcome to visit again." From the father's perspective, he feels much more confident in his friend. Now that Prakash has had a glimpse of Raj's business skills, Prakash is less worried about Raj.

"Who cares if he wants to manage a small hotel in Goa."

"He seems to be good at business, and it makes him happy."

"Not everyone needs fame and fortune to get on with life."

"I just hope that he settles down soon before it is too late. But that is his business, not mine."

These are the thoughts that fill his mind of late when it comes to his dear friend.

Meena pours Anika a glass of water. Raj senses Anika's change of demeanour, and he too begins to become sentimental and tear up a bit, "I will miss you all. More than you know."

Raj then stands. "If you'll kindly excuse me, I have some last-minute things to take care of. Goodnight, everyone."

The guest walks out of the dining room and heads back to the pool house. His feet feel heavy under his body, and his heart feels strained in his chest. He did not expect his news at dinner to have such an effect on the family or on himself. Even so, he knows his decision is for the best.

The Marlin

Later that evening, Raj is back in the pool house, and he is now ready to call it a day. And what a day it has been! He sits on the side of his bed and looks over his phone, deep in thought. Raj has a text message typed out. And he debates whether to send it.

The text message reads: "Anika, I'm sorry that I have to go. Please know that you will be missed. Thank you for all the wonderful experiences that we enjoyed together."

After pondering for a few moments, Raj deletes the 'Please know that you will be missed' part. He then presses send on his phone, and he places it down next to his pillow.

Almost immediately, he gets the following response: "Loser."

Raj reads the message and places the phone down again. He now becomes emotional and feels despair in his heart. Raj looks across the room at the door leading outside. He contemplates what to do next and just as he is about to stand, the cover of a novel on the bookshelf next to the bed catches his eye.

It is the first book on the third row, and from where he sits, Raj eyes the cover with penetrating eyes. The book is *The Old Man and the Sea*. Raj remembers reading it as a teenager. But it has been decades since he has glanced at anything else from Hemmingway. Even so, Raj recalls this particular story well. The story is of an aging fisherman who struggles against defeat to catch a magnificent but evasive marlin. In the end, the withering old man does manage to haul in the incredible fish. But only after sacrificing everything along the way, including the great marlin itself. Even so, the protagonist emerges as a hero. Raj recalls this much very well.

As a youth, Raj drew great inspiration from the fisherman that battled all odds in pursuit of his destiny. But now as he stares back out at the door, Raj wonders if the old man in the novel was too steadfast and even foolhardy in a world where death is inevitable, but solitude is not.

Yet sitting on the bed, Raj's legs refuse to move. Something deeper keeps him from standing up. His heart wants to race out the door, but his body feels an intense force pulling him back. So after some time, Raj gives in to gravity, and he lies his back down. Raj turns off the light and stares up at the ceiling. But his mind is unable to reach any meaningful conclusions. And he does not invite his heart to the conversation.

The Sacrifice

Later that evening, Anika walks up to the door of her mother's room. The young lady begins to knock on the door but pauses for a second. And then she goes to knock again. But she pauses for another second. Finally, Anika knocks on the door.

Prakash is downstairs in his office, and Meena is already in bed. The mother shouts out from the other side, "Yes? Anika, is that you?"

"Yes, Mommy," Anika calls out.

"Come on in, dear. What's going on?"

Anika enters the room; she looks pensive and even nervous.

"Are you not sleepy? You've had a long day, I imagine." The mother motions her daughter to come and sit by her side of the bed.

"No. Well, yes. I don't know. I guess my brain is running on overtime, but my body is running on fumes." The daughter rests on the front of the bed and faces the door, but then she turns to face her mother.

"Is there anything you want to tell me, Anika?"

"Well, it's just that... Oh, nothing, really." She manages to whisper. Anika wants to tell her mother about her feelings for Raj, but she cannot bring herself to broach the topic. At this point, her emotions are so engulfed that she just wants to run away from everything.

"Anika?"

After a pause, "I've been thinking of doing some traveling. Seeing more of the country. Not now, of course, but sometime soon... in the future."

"That's out of the blue. What prompted this?" This news causes the mother to sit up straight.

"Not sure. I've just been thinking, perhaps there's more to the world that I have yet to see and experience."

At first, this vexes the mother, "Your father wants you to concentrate on your career, young lady."

"Yes, but my career will always be there."

"Are you sure? You aren't getting any younger, dear," Meena retorts with a stern expression on her face.

"That's what I mean. I feel like there's this entire world out there that I don't know much about," the young lady's voice pleads.

"Anika, it's not in our culture to have a young lady like yourself go traveling around the country all alone."

"Haven't you ever wanted to just get away from everything?" The daughter tries to look for common ground.

"Of course, everybody does. But we have responsibilities that must come first." Meena's internal worry-meter spikes. Her voice strains. The dialogue shifts from a conversation to a single-sided argument. And anxiety gets the best of Meena. The mother is too ruffled to stay in bed, so she begins to pace the room, in front of where Anika is sitting.

A million thoughts of what could happen to her daughter spiral through her mind. "There is no way a young lady should travel on her own like this," the mother thinks to herself.

At this point, Anika realizes that her mother is not listening any longer. This frustrates the daughter, so she retreats to silence. But she continues to look her mother in the eye for an opening.

Meena's diatribe continues after a pause, and over this period, she becomes more and more worked up. But soon, most of her words only come out in spurts and streaks.

"Who would take care of your father?"

"Who would take care of you?"

"In society, one can't just run off and do whatever they want, whenever they want."

"There would be chaos."

After some time, the mother finally runs out of breath. This gives Anika a chance to respond. "But you only live once, mother. Do you not have any regrets?"

Without thinking, the mother is rapid to respond, "No, I've always put my family first. The happiness of my family is worth more than my happiness."

"Are you sure? No regrets at all?" The daughter presses back.

The matriarch sees the strain in her daughter's eyes for the first time. And in them, the mother notices despair and sorrow. This touches Meena to the core and causes the mother to take a step back.

She regains a little composure and then responds, this time in a softer tone. "Listen, Anika, we all have regrets. It's just that there's only so much you can do. I've sacrificed my life for this family. How could I regret that? After all, obligations must be met. This is our culture. This is our tradition. Family comes first. And without culture, without tradition, we have nothing."

Anika capitulates, realizing she's not getting anywhere. She appreciates that her mother is less exasperated. Even so, the daughter knows her mother well. When she has made up her mind on something, there is no convincing her otherwise.

The young lady whispers back as she stands to leave, "Okay, Mommy."

"You'll understand when you get older, dear."

Anika starts walking back to her room. While she is in the hallway, she rereads her previous text, just as she is about to open her door. The young lady gasps out loud and drops her phone to the ground. The spectacle is so loud that she likely woke the whole house. She swipes up her phone and jumps into her room and slams the door behind herself.

The Madras Coffee

Before even turning on the light to her room, Anika types out the first thing that comes to her mind. "OMG. I meant to say, 'Lousy.' Raj, I'm sorry to see you go as well. I also had a wonderful time getting to know you. Please understand that I will miss you."

The young lady clicks send and then collapses on to her bed in tears. All she wants to do at this point is to disappear. She thinks of all the children in the orphanage and how they do not have a fraction of the opportunity that she has had. She knows that she grew up with a silver spoon in her mouth. Even so, Anika still feels trapped. "If only I could start over. Fresh as an emerging butterfly," she thinks to herself.

The daughter places her head on her pillow, and she stares up at the ceiling. But her heart is unable to reach any meaningful conclusions. And he does not invite her mind to the conversation. And so she does not fall asleep until the first swallows begin to cheer on the sun on its way to work.

On the morning of the following day, Raj rolls out of his bed. He begins to pack his bag and tidy the room. Raj has not slept well either, and his stomach feels tight, and his chest is sore. But as he packs, Raj receives a text from Anika.

"Be sure to have a final Madras coffee before you leave town."

"Will try. Going to be a busy day."

"For me too. Lots of errands to run."

Anika and Raj text throughout the day. Each tries to think of an excuse to meet the other, but for some reason or another, they cannot connect face-to-face.

More than once, Raj wonders if he has feelings for the young woman. But each time, before he can finish the thought, his mind convinces him otherwise. "Maybe in another life," Raj thinks to himself.

The Hug

It is now evening. Raj comes back from running errands, and he enters the pool house.

As soon as the guest places his shopping bag on the floor, he receives a message from Anika. "Too busy to say hello?"

Raj replies, "Not at all. I saw that all the lights were out at home. Is anyone home?"

"My parents are out to dinner with friends. I'm in my room."

"Come on over."

"I'm catching up on some reading."

"I'm about to crack open a KF. Care for an apple martini?"

The young lady is reluctant about this. She wants to meet him, but she is afraid of what may come out of her mouth. For the entire day, she has been experiencing a mix of frustration, anger, and fear. "I should get some work done." She looks out of her window, and she sees the moon, bright and awake. "There's nothing good that can come of me visiting him," Anika thinks to herself.

"I'm sure your work will be there when you return. If you're worried, just lock your work in your desk. That way, it won't run away from you."

"Right." After a pause, she capitulates. "Okay, I'll be down in a few."

When Anika arrives, Raj is sitting by the chair to the left of the side table with the chess pieces on it. He takes another sip of his KF as the young lady makes her way towards the empty chair next to him. Her martini is waiting on the side table, guarded by a sea of pawns.

Soft instrumental music to the tune of *Lag Ja Gale* plays in the background.

Raj calls out to her as she enters, "It's a beautiful night."

He spent the day walking around Mumbai, reliving many of the fond memories that he built up over the past month. And although he wishes he could stay, Raj knows better. The businessman understands that Goa is where he belongs, and he resigns himself to his fate.

Still, Raj is grateful to have reconnected with his friend. And he will never forget all the people that he has met here, especially the young lady standing before him.

"The moon is out," Anika manages to say after a lengthy pause. At this point, the young lady is not only physically exhausted but also mentally fatigued. The entire day Anika has been thinking about how to say goodbye to Raj. But no matter what the young lady comes up with, nothing seems to fit her emotions.

Raj passes her the cocktail. "Here, to a lasting friendship. Cheers."

"Cheers. Off to bigger and better things," Anika utters back.

"Right. Listen, I want you to know, I will miss you dearly." Raj looks her in the eyes while saying this. He feels at peace having come to terms with his situation. But at the same time, he understands that this situation cannot be comfortable for the young lady either. He notices that she is shaking, but also that she is trying her best to maintain her composure.

"Well, can I at least get a hug before you leave?" She now peers into his eyes for solace.

"Sure. You can hug me, but it wouldn't be appropriate for me to hug you."

He stands, and Raj puts his arms in the air. "Hug away."

Anika rises and folds her arms around his chest. Without thinking, she kisses him on his neck. She whispers, "I love you. I'll miss you so much."

Raj puts down his hands and lifts her face towards his. Raj sees tears begin to swell in her eyes and empathizes with her feelings of longing. Also, without thinking, he kisses her forehead.

After a moment's pause, they continue to look into each other's eyes. Finally, they both lean in to kiss each other. But before either of them can make sense of what is happening, an engine roars from outside. It is an automobile, and it pulls into the driveway of the home.

"I have to go, Raj."

The car screeches to an abrupt halt, and the engine cuts off.

"I know."

Anika makes a rapid exit, but it is clear that her face is full of tears as she runs out of the pool house door.

The Pearl

Meena enters the home, and she waves goodbye to her husband in the car in the driveway. The wife takes off her shawl and hangs it in the closet.

Earlier that evening, her husband received a page from the emergency room. He was second on call, but the first doctor ended up in an accident on the way to the hospital.

"Looks like I have no choice on this one," Prakash peers up from his pager. "My sincere apologies, Mr. Dalal. I am very sorry, Mrs. Dalal, we'll have to do this again soon."

The doctor stands from the table, and he shakes the hands of his dinner guests.

"After twenty-five years, this never gets old," Meena smiles back.

"I'll drop you home on my way to the hospital, dear," Prakash suggests.

"So sorry we have to leave early you two," Meena stands as well and the two depart.

Meena steps up the staircase and walks down the hallway to her room. "It's good to be back home," she thinks to herself.

As the mother approaches her bedroom door, Anika paces forward at the end of the hallway. The daughter tries to hide in the shadows. But the mother sees her feet in the light from the window at the end of the hall. Meena takes slow, even steps, and she begins to approach Anika. The daughter feels sad and even distressed. But Meena doesn't notice at first, given the darkness and distance between them.

"Hello, dear," Meena says. "I must say these dinners are becoming less and less exciting over the years. Anika, are you heading to the kitchen? Mind grabbing my purse? I left it on the counter."

The mother continues to walk towards Anika, who now has paused at the other end of the hallway. Meena continues, "Your father spilled his drink on his tie, so I'll need to rinse it in the sink. The Dalals can be so tiring. Always going on about some new and crazy real estate deal. Luckily, the hospital called your father away on a case. But oh my, can they go on and on and on. Vivek is as exciting as dried mud, and Isha is always lost in her own fantasy world."

As she approaches her daughter, Meena notices her distress. "What's wrong, dear?"

Anika proceeds to fall into her mother's arms, and she begins to cry over Meena's shoulder. After a break in her crying, the daughter starts to speak through her tears. "I'm lost. I just can't."

"You can't what, dear? Tell me what's wrong." The mother leads her into the master bedroom.

Meanwhile, Raj finds Anika's necklace on the carpet near the foot of the side table. It is a thin gold chain with a small round pearl, shiny and white, at its centre. He picks it up. And he holds it to the light, and so it sparkles. He then drops the necklace in the palm of his other hand and then proceeds to the house to return the lost item.

"Mommy, what do you and Daddy want from me?" The daughter is still crying.

"To be happy, of course. Please tell me what's bothering you, dear," Meena consoles.

"Mommy, Raj is going soon, and I can't bear to see him leave. I'll miss him so much," Anika continues.

Meena is taken aback, but she holds her composure. "Anika, what are you trying to tell me?"

"Mommy, I think I'm in love with him."

Without missing a beat, the mother leads her daughter to the bed and sits her down. "Sit down, dear. I'll be okay. Tell me what's going on."

"I can't go on without him. What do I do?"

The mother places her hand on Anika's and responds with sincerity. "Listen, I know that you've become very fond of Raj, but do you know how he feels about you?"

Anika is still crying but is now somewhat calmer. "He treats me like an equal. Raj respects my opinion, and we have so much in common. I'm not sure if I'll ever meet anyone like him again. And I'm not sure if I'll ever get to see him again."

At that moment, mother and daughter look towards Prakash's photo on the nightstand. Meena then continues, "I see."

Around this time, Raj passes through the living room and makes his way up the steps. He then walks down the hallway towards the master bedroom. Raj pauses outside the master bedroom. From outside the door, he hears the mother and daughter talking inside.

Anika continues, "I know the kind of son-in-law Daddy has in mind. A young, well-settled surgeon. Someone from a wealthy family, ready and waiting to take over his practice. But that's just not for me. I want someone who will be my best friend. I want someone I can share all my deepest cares and fears with, and someone who really cares what I think and how I feel. I'm not ready to settle down, start having kids, and never see the world outside of this city. Mommy, what am I to do?"

Without stopping to think, Meena responds. "But in society..." and then she pauses for a few seconds. The mother then gives a big sigh of resignation. "Okay, dear. Let me talk to your father."

At this point, Raj begins to move forward towards the room. But just before he's about to enter, he stops himself and decides to go back to his room. As Raj walks back down the hallway, he drops the necklace on top of the side table in the hall.

The Crashing Chair

The next morning, the family is in the kitchen for breakfast. Prakash sits across from Meena, and Anika is on the far end of the table. Both mother and daughter look exhausted after an emotional night. But Prakash is energetic and rested.

The father reaches across the table for the butter and begins to butter his toast. "I have some good news."

Meena is still half-asleep. She pretends to read her magazine. But she cannot concentrate enough to read the words on the page, given that she feels so tired. She responds with a yawn. "What's that, dear?"

The father continues. "I did my first case with Dr. Rahul Khanna last night. I'm more than impressed with the boy. He just finished his residency a few years ago, and he has the hands of a skilled artist."

The mother is unable to match her husband's excitement. "That's wonderful, dear."

"I'm really impressed," he states again. "Dr. Khanna joined two weeks ago, and he's already close with all the staff. His training is superb, and it turns out I know his family very well. His uncle was a professor at my medical school. Boy, was he tough!"

"I'm glad you've met a new friend, Prakash. Let's have dinner with him and his wife sometime."

The doctor continues. "That's just it. I found out after our operation that he's single. Meena, I would like to propose Anika to him."

At this point, both the mother and daughter look up at the same time. In an instant, they give their full attention to Prakash. Both of them now wear worried expressions across their faces.

The father (not expecting such a response) begins to defend himself. "It's been years since we've had someone so proficient join our medical staff. I think we're getting better at recruiting talent."

Anika looks at Meena, who in turn looks from Anika to Prakash, unsure how to proceed. Now, Raj walks into the kitchen, with his backpack all packed.

Raj places the bag near the entrance of the kitchen and takes a seat across from the young lady. "Good morning, everyone. Looks like I'm off to a late start on my last day."

"Morning, Raj. Come sit. Have some chai." The doctor waves his friend over. "Apparently, I'm the only one with some energy this morning."

"So it seems." Raj looks around the table and notices the subdued looks on Meena and Anika's faces. As he sits down, he grabs a *samosa* and places it on the plate in front of him. Raj takes another look around the table. "Is everything okay?"

Prakash begins after a pause, "I think everyone is waiting for their coffee to kick in. I was just mentioning my new colleague to Meena and Anika. He's a wonderful young man. I think he would be a great match for my daughter."

All Raj can do is give his head a slight nod. Yet, his countenance turns from placid to worry as his understanding comes up to speed with the others in the room.

Without noticing the change in the demeanour of his friend, the father continues. "Dr. Khanna is a fine kid. Raj, you should come back for the engagement and for the wedding. You'll have a splendid time, I'm sure of it."

At this point, Meena feels compelled to speak up. She reaches across the table and puts her hand on Prakash's. "Prakash, it could be that your daughter already has somebody in mind. Please think long term. She needs to make the final decision on who to marry."

Yet the husband does not understand his wife's line of thinking. "Yes, yes. Of course, Anika will get the final say. This is the twenty-first century, after all. There's nothing to worry about."

The mother continues, "That's not what I mean, Prakash. What if Anika already has someone else in mind?"

This shocks Prakash, given that the thought is so unexpected. He is then quick to lose his temper, and barks back, "What are you talking about? Anika, what is your mother trying to tell me."

For some reason, all Anika can do is shake her head back and forth, almost in disbelief of the entire situation.

The father becomes dismayed at this point. "Meena, tell me what you're talking about. I demand to know! Identify the boy. Why haven't you told me before!"

As the situation has come to this point, the mother sees no choice but to point at Raj.

Prakash turns towards Raj. "Do you know who she's talking about?" The father seems to suspect that Raj is in on something with his wife and daughter. "Raj, tell me the truth. Who is this person that my daughter is interested in?"

"It's me," Raj whispers.

At first, Prakash misunderstands his friend. "Ismeet? I don't believe you. The ophthalmologist? Isn't he divorced?"

Ramla, with his back facing the family, as he is cooking over the stove, chimes in. "No, he's separated, not divorced. He does have two kids, though."

The patriarch is furious, and he looks around the table for answers. Prakash then looks towards Anika. "Two kids! Anika, where did you meet Ismeet? What have you gotten yourself into? Tell me right now."

Meena tries to step in. "It's not Ismeet Khan. Prakash, try to control yourself."

But the father cannot control himself. He is beyond consoling now "Then who? Tell me!"

Before the daughter is forced to respond, Raj steps in. "Prakash, I'm the one. I am interested in your daughter."

Prakash pushes his chair back, he jumps to his feet. As he's standing up, the chair falls backward and hits the ground with a loud crash. The father then stares into his friend's eyes, and he slaps him hard, without thinking.

Raj doesn't move, but he does try to explain the situation. "Prakash, listen."

"You traitor!" The yell is loud enough to echo across the home. Unable to control himself and overcome with contempt, Prakash slaps Raj again. "How dare you! You are my guest—my close friend. I did not expect this from you. You're just a small hotel owner without a formal education. What could you possibly give to Anika?"

Without looking away, Raj continues to stare deep into Prakash's eyes. "I can only give her respect and happiness."

"What kind of relationship would that be? This is not possible," Prakash shouts.

"It would be a union built upon love and respect," Raj replies.

"Enough! I want you to leave this house as soon as possible and never come back again." The father pounds his foot on the ground.

Raj realizes that he will not be able to convince his friend, so he gives a firm nod back to the patriarch. "As you wish."

Meena and Anika give pleading stares to Prakash. And so does the rest of the staff, including Ramla, Mangla, Ramu, and even Sughandha, who have all now gathered in the kitchen after the commotion. Raj walks over to his backpack, and he picks it up. He places the bag over his right shoulder.

Raj then walks up to Meena and takes his blessings from her. "Thank you for being such a gracious host. I know I've outstayed my welcome, but I'll never forget your hospitality."

The mother holds back her emotions with a frown. She feels powerless, and she now has tears in her eyes. In fact, the entire kitchen has become saddened and emotional, except for the hostile father. Prakash stands with his arms crossed, breathing heavy breaths as if he is trying not to hyperventilate.

Raj places his hands together and bows to Ramu, Sughandha, Ramla, and Mangla. "Thank you all for making my stay comfortable. You are all special to me. Each one of you means more to me than you will ever know."

They all bow back, with tears in their eyes.

Finally, Raj stops in front of Anika. She does not have tears in her eyes, but rather, she has a look of resolve and faith. Raj gazes into her eyes, and he tells her, "Be well. But I know you well and everything will work out. Please tell me once you've finalized your wedding date. I'll be sure to make it to the *mangala sutra ceremony* and the *sindoor* ceremony." Many consider this first ceremony, where the husband ties a necklace around the bride's neck, to be the most important when it comes to Hindu weddings. Others consider the *sindoor* ceremony to be even more important, for it is during this ceremony where the husband first places an orange-red coloured dot on his wife.

Raj turns towards Prakash, who now also has tears in his eyes. But the father's arms are still crossed in front of his chest. Raj gives an almost imperceptible nod and then turns and walks out the front door.

At that moment, Anika's cell phone rings. The young lady looks down at the phone. It is Neha (the call centre girl). She hangs up on her and then looks up at Raj and gives him a broad smile. Raj returns her smile and proceeds to walk out the door.

As he leaves, Sughandha calls out to him, "We'll miss you, Raj!" This was the first time that most can remember

Sughandha saying so much, and in front of so many people. But she too has a broad smile on her face. And tears roll down her cheeks as she waves goodbye to Raj.

This action unites the rest of the family to also call out to the departing guest, "We'll miss you, Raj!" they all say, almost in unison.

The Eggplant

Raj steps out of the home. The sun is hiding, and clouds fill the sky. And it is dark and overcast. And the swallows are not singing either. A light rain fills the air with a heavy mist. Raj takes a coin from his pocket. He flicks it into the sparking water-filled basin as he walks past the fountain. He then pulls out his phone to check the time and notices that his battery is dead. "Just my luck," Raj thinks to himself.

Then thunder strikes. And heavy rain fills the air. Water begins to fall from the sky as if a dam broke from above the heavens. Raj thinks to himself, "When was the last time it rained like this?"

The departing guest takes one last look at the home behind him. He takes a deep breath, and after a long pause, he then makes his way towards the front gate. A large poplar provides shelter to the left of the entrance, so Raj takes refuge as best he can. But it is too late. In the minute that he has been outdoors, Raj has become soaked from head to toe. He considers using his backpack for cover. But Raj finds it useless as the rain interrogates him from all sides, even from under the tree. As he waits there for advice from the heavens, Raj hears someone call his name from behind.

Raj looks back towards the house, but only sees a dark figure approaching him. Raj cannot see who it is. The heavy-set man runs towards Raj with swift strides and intensity. This causes water to splash around in all directions. Whoever it is, he looks scary and determined. And he is wielding a long instrument, that could very well be a sword or a lance. "Here we go," thinks the soaked gentleman, who drops his bag and clenches his fists, but mostly to keep warm.

As the figure approaches, Raj recognizes the face. It is Ramu. And he is holding not a lance, but an umbrella.

"Didn't think you would get too far without this," the chauffeur hands it over.

"You know, you could have used this yourself."

"I know. But anyway, I need a shower."

"Thank you, Ramu."

"Do take care, Raj. Do take care."

Raj opens the umbrella, picks up his bag, and turns to leave. But before moving, he gives Ramu a heartfelt salute. Raj than walks out of the gate and down the street. But he decides to take cover under the vegetable stand at the corner of the road. It is here that he encounters the father and son duo, Rustom and Billu. They are buying eggplant, and Rustom is paying the vendor.

Raj's eyes are swollen, given that he had been crying. Raj approaches the father and son, and they recognize him this time.

Rustom calls out, "I see you have rain in your eyes. Here, take this." The father pulls out a napkin from the vegetable stand's countertop and hands it to Raj.

Raj takes the napkin and wipes his eyes and nose. "Thank you, Rustom."

"Doing well today, Billu?" Raj inquires, now that he's cleared his face with the napkin.

"Okay," Billu responds.

"Where you headed, young man?"

"Station."

"How about a ride? I got her back yesterday. They found my car, two blocks from my home. Can you believe it?" the father points to his car.

"That would be great. Thank you, Rustom."

The Thunder

Back at home, Meena and Prakash are upstairs in their bedroom. The rain pours from the outside the window, and lightning strikes every few minutes. The wife confronts the husband about what happened at breakfast.

"Prakash, I expect more from you." Meena's eyes rage with fire.

"I am only looking out for my daughter's well-being. I have from the moment she was born, and I will continue until the moment I die." The husband feels defiant and combative.

"You know very well what I mean, Prakash." The wife scolds.

"Why am I in the wrong? I can't believe my good friend has done this to me after all this time. What did I ever do to him to deserve this?" This makes the husband feel defensive, and he takes a step back away from the bed, where Meena is standing. His ego is not only hurt, but it is also smouldering.

"Prakash, now stop it. Don't be selfish. This is not about you and your burnt ego. This is about the happiness of our daughter."

The patriarch feels offended. "What do you mean? That's all I'm concerned about—about what's best for Anika. There's nothing more important than having a stable marriage. I cannot let this proposal go. Dr. Khanna is one-in-a-million. He'll take over my practice, I'm sure. I can't think of a better son-in-law. His uncle is very well known, you know."

The mother counters again with a stern expression on her face. "See what I mean, Prakash? This is not about you and your practice, and whatever legacy you're trying to create. Our daughter has been trying to tell you all this time that she wants something else out of life. And all her desires have been falling on deaf ears."

"You misunderstand me completely." His tone lightens, and his voice quavers, but his mood begins to soften. But only by an imperceptible amount.

"Come on, be honest with yourself for once. You're not going for a marriage. You're going for a conditional union with self-centred intentions. Let me remind you of when we got married. You know very well the main reason you pursued me was to get into my father's practice."

"I made that very clear to your father the day I approached him. I hid nothing of my intentions."

"I didn't say you did. What I'm saying is that there's more to life than calculated alliances. Marriage is not a game of chess. That's not what makes a wife happy, or what makes a family content."

"Are you not happy? What about the house, the cars, the servants, the luxurious vacations, and the fancy parties?"

"Marriage is not about acquiring the most chess pieces, the fanciest cars, and the biggest house. A union is about two things—respect and love. That's what Raj has for Anika."

Prakash is unable to control himself. "Enough! I don't want to hear any more of this. I know what's best for my daughter, and my word is final!"

The father then storms out of the bedroom without allowing Meena to reply. As he slams the door shut, thunder and lightning fill the sky as if this last strike is meters away from the house.

The Beach House

The next day, Raj arrives back to his hometown of Goa. The city has a different feel from Mumbai. Goa is more like a relaxed beach town as compared to the hustle and bustle of Mumbai. The street outside the train station where Raj arrives at is busy with tourists and vendors to accommodate them. Instead of household goods and vegetables, these stands sell t-shirts and trinkets. But everyone seems to move at a slower pace, with no intention of going anywhere in particular.

Raj's clothes are now dry, but his backpack is damp and soggy. Raj keeps it inside a plastic shopping bag, which he now carries on his arm. Once he arrives, the traveller looks up and down the road and considers his next move.

But near the entrance of the station, a thin and tall man comes up to Raj from behind. He taps on Raj's shoulder and as Raj turns around the man gives Raj a warm, loving hug. "Welcome home, Raj."

"Good to be home, brother," Raj replies.

"You look like you need to get some rest," Ram Iqbal continues. "You must be exhausted from the trip."

"I'm okay, brother."

"Listen, Raj, Anika already called and told me what happened. I assured her I would take good care of you. So for now, it's best you get some rest."

Raj agrees. "You're right. I'll need some time to myself. I'll actually head to Papa's house for now."

It is clear that the traveller wants to get away from things, and his father's old beach house is isolated enough to allow such an escape.

"As you wish. I'll have dinner sent over once you've had some time to rest."

"Thanks. Tell me, what did I miss? Can I help with anything?"

"Don't you worry. The business isn't going anywhere, I assure you."

Raj smiles and nods. "Thank you, Ram Iqbal. It's good to be back."

The Cat

Over the next few weeks, everyone goes back to their regular routines.

Prakash tries to keep himself busy at the hospital. He stops all work with the temple, though. Raj's footprints are all over the project, and the doctor cannot make himself face such a task. Given that he still feels betrayed by his friend, the doctor shelves the initiative. The last thing he wants is to come upon an issue where he would need to reach out to his former friend.

Yet over this period, the father continues to grow fonder of the young surgeon. Dr. Khanna is ambitious and steadfast. "What more could a father-in-law want?" he thinks to himself.

There is a proud look on Prakash's face whenever he handles medical cases with the young man. "If only he had joined my practice a year ago. All this nonsense could have been avoided," he tells Meena one evening.

The wife is busy tending to her garden at the front of the house. "You never let up, do you, Prakash?" Meena takes off her garden gloves. She then begins to water the plants with the hose, which she takes from Ramu, who is washing the car behind her.

The chauffeur rinses the sponge out into the bucket of soapy water. "Of course, the doctor doesn't let up. Even on his days off, his mind keeps going." The driver gives Meena a wink.

"Maybe we need to find my husband a second job? He has too much free time on his hands. Can you teach him to wash cars? I'm afraid he'll drown my vegetables when they don't follow his commands to grow faster."

"Have you considered fishing, sir? You can bring home dinner for Ramla to cook up each night with Meena's yummy vegetables."

"Very funny, you too," Prakash grumbles.

Anika goes back to volunteering at the orphanage after convincing Gaurav to take her back. In truth, the place was a mess since she left. But the boss keeps this fact to himself when the young lady returns. Yet soon after, a full-time, paid position opens up. The young lady is quick to seize the opportunity and now works there full-time.

After her first week back, she helps an elderly lady adopt one of the older boys in the home. But at first, her boss is vehement in opposing the match. "We prefer younger parents. And who will be his father in all this? This is not our custom, Anika."

"Arun is thirteen years old. This child has a once-in-a-lifetime opportunity to start a new life. And the elderly lady loves him like a first-born child. And if he stays in this place any longer, we'll lose him forever. I know this deep in my heart," Anika pleads.

"When I brought you onto our staff, I did not expect for you turn all our rules upside down, young lady," Gaurav retorts. The old man has been with the orphanage for over twenty-five years. And over this entire time, their rules have never changed. "Children belong with a husband and a wife. It is only natural."

"It is not natural to have children without parents. But here we are. We must face the fact that not everyone will live a fantasy life," she insists. "Look, if Arun were your child, you would want the best for him. And I know, he is far better off with Latima even though she is sixty, then in here, where he has no one. In a few years, he'll be on the streets. Another statistic. Is that what you want?"

Anika takes her case to the board of directors. The board then invites her to speak to them in person. They are so impressed by her passionate yet rational plea that they agree with her proposal on the spot.

The Hi-Fi Club continues to frequent the Madras Leaf Café. This evening they are enjoying afternoon tea. Dhansukh oversees them, and this time, he has a big smile on his face. The group cut a deal with the Café. All Club meetings going forward will be held at the Café, and the Club will receive a 30% discount on drinks. "It's a win-win, the way I see it," Dhansukh explains to the owner.

"Good work, son. Keep it up!" the owner places his heavy hand on the manager's shoulder.

Raj returns to leading his business affairs from his father's old beach cottage. From his busy desk, he places phone calls, works through contracts, meets with vendors. He also does not stop to rest much.

One day, Ram Iqbal walks into his office and hands him an envelope. Raj (still on the phone) smiles, takes the letter and places it on his desk. The correspondence reads, "Last Will and Testament." Ram Iqbal exits the room, so as not to disturb the phone call.

Rustom and Billu vacation by the pool of a beach resort, drinking out of coconuts. The father wears a bathing suit. The son dons a black t-shirt and jeans. And next to Billu is a third person. A young lady who is also wearing a black t-shirt and jeans. But she is sipping a piña colada. And all three guests wear back, thick-framed sunglasses. And on the two black t-shirts, in large white letters are two words, "Just Married."

Suffice it to say, "life goes on," Sughandha thinks to herself. She puts down her book and begins to play with Tolstoy, the new family pet. The young kitten wandered into the home the day after Raj departed, and Ramla has prepared him fresh delicacies every day since. Tolstoy now lives in the pool house, where he reads books and plays chess. Or at least the feline does his best to pretend to enjoy such things.

The Pitch

The family is having dinner, yet things are not the same as they used to be. Everyone is still somewhat morose as if mourning the loss of a loved one.

Prakash breaks the silence. "Good to see you back at work, Anika. Doesn't it feel good to be productive?"

"I guess so, Daddy," The daughter responds as she tries to fake a smile.

"Well," the father continues, "I know this is a sore topic for you, young lady, but do your father a favour, will you?"

Meena looks up with a stern look on her face as she stares back at her husband.

Anika knows what's coming next, but rather than make a big issue, she gives lets out a big sigh of resignation instead. "What's that, Daddy?"

"Please meet Rahul," Prakash says with care. "There's nothing wrong with meeting him. If you don't like him, you'll never have to see him again. I promise."

"Okay, Daddy."

Prakash puts his hand on his daughter's and smiles with appreciation. "That's my girl. I love you, dear."

Anika responds with a flat expression. "I love you too, Daddy."

The Envelope

Raj is in his office, and he sits at his desk with his head immersed in a stack of contracts. Towers of paper now consume not only his desk but also every open surface in the room.

"If paper could reproduce on its own, this is what the world would look like," Ram Iqbal thinks to himself as he enters.

The phone on Raj's desk rings every few minutes. Each time this happens, the boss picks it up, replies with a few words, and then he hangs up. Ram Iqbal walks towards his half-brother's desk. He's carrying a letter, which he hands to Raj. The boss takes the correspondence and places it on his stack of papers, almost without noticing it.

"Would you like a sandwich?" Ram Iqbal inquires.

"No, thanks. I'll eat something later," Raj replies without giving any formal acknowledgment.

"Have you ever had breakfast?"

The boss pauses for a moment. He considers the word 'breakfast' as if he is hearing the concept for the first time. Raj then continues reading the document in front of him, marking up the text with the pen in his hand. "No, I guess not."

"It's almost mid-day. You must eat something. I see that you haven't even touched your morning chai."

"Yes, you're right. I'll eat in a bit. Listen, have you seen the latest draft for the new construction project?"

"The paralegal returned it yesterday. Yes, it is now reviewed, and it is ready to sign. Raj, why don't you take a break? It's the weekend, and you haven't stopped working, or even left this office in almost two weeks. What's the big rush?"

"No rush. You either get busy living, or you get busy dying."

"You call this living? There's an entire world out there, and you haven't even seen the light of day in who knows how long."

"I'm just catching up on lost time. Not to worry. I'll be up to speed soon."

"Life is not a race, Raj," Ram Iqbal interrupts.

This latest comment gives Raj pause. But only for a second. Before finishing his current breath, the boss resumes his work.

"Why don't you take a minute and check out the letter that arrived from Mumbai? I'm sure you'll find it quite interesting."

Raj reaches for the envelope. He looks at the front of the correspondence and notices the address. The boss gives a questioning look to his brother, who nods his head in affirmation. Raj then opens the letter and sees that it is an invitation.

Dr. & Mrs. Prakash Malhotra

Solicit the honour of your gracious presence at the marriage of their daughter

Anika

to

Rahul

Son of Dr. & Mrs. Bhavin Khanna

Friday, the Thirteenth of March

(Reception to follow)

The boss looks up at Ram Iqbal. "It's Anika's wedding invitation. She's marrying Dr. Khanna at the end of the month, on the thirtieth."

"I'll get your suit ready. Shall I book transportation?"

"Not yet, Ram Iqbal. Not yet."

Not sure what to make of the invitation, Raj places it back in the envelope. He then puts it on the stack of papers on the right-hand side of his desk. The boss looks around the room as if to contemplate something important. It looks like he is mulling something over, but even he is unclear what to make of the situation. A moment later, Raj picks up the document he was working on before the interruption, and he begins to mark it up again.

"Very well," Ram Iqbal calls out. The brother turns around and heads out of the room. He closes the door behind him, leaving Raj once again alone in the office, busy at work.

The Phone Call

Sughandha sits at her favourite spot in the home. She is next to the bookcase in the living room of the Malhotra family. And she wears headphones and listens to classical music. Tolstoy lays with a lazy smile on her lap while she consumes the novel between her hands.

She is reading *Love in the Time of Cholera* by Gabriel García Márquez. Fermina Daza is the protagonist of the novel if there is one. And she has waited over fifty years for the man that she first loved to return into her life. "How many things in life are worth waiting this long for?" Sughandha wonders to herself as she rubs her hand across Tolstoy's back.

The woman then takes off her headphones. And as she does this, her soul fills with beautiful, vibrant festive music playing in the living room. The rest of the home is in celebration mode. It is a few days before the big wedding. And today, the family is holding an engagement ceremony.

Colourful flowers, dominated by red and pink, combined with auspicious décor, fill the home. The priest has finished the *puja* to invoke, welcome, honour the gods. And Anika and Rahul go through the various steps of the ceremony.

The groom seems confident, yet he is also stern and stoic. The bride appears to be pensive and saddened. And from time to time, the young lady looks at her phone by her side with a sense of urgency, as if she is commanding for it to ring.

Prakash is busy directing the staff. Meena is welcoming the guests. Ramu is entertaining them. And Mangla is serving snacks prepared by Ramla earlier in the day.

In the middle of the ceremony, Anika's phone rings. Her phone says, "Unknown Caller," and she is rapid to pick it up. "Hello?"

"Hello, Duchess Anika. This is Neha from New Fashion Stores. I've been trying to reach you regarding your deposit refund. We notice that you never cashed your check."

Anika cuts her off and snaps back a reply, "Donate it." She hangs up. The young lady's stomach is in knots, and she has not eaten much all day. Rahul gives her a questioning stare, but she dismisses his looks.

The ceremony continues.

The Wakeup Call

Three days later, Ram Iqbal enters Raj's office. From the door to the office, the room appears to be empty. But as Ram Iqbal walks around the boss's desk, he finds that he is asleep in his chair. The disk is so buried in papers that the brother cannot even see the sleeping body until he is close enough to hear the snoring.

Ram Iqbal places the chai and biscuits on the table and taps the boss on the shoulder. "Raj, you do have a bed, you know."

The boss wakes up, his hair a mess, and he now has a beard. "What day is it?"

"It's Friday."

Raj is half-asleep; he sits back in his chair and looks back at the brother, deflated and weary. The boss cannot keep his eyes open for more than a few seconds at a time.

"Have some chai," Ram Iqbal offers. "How about you take a long shower? It'll wake you up."

"Ram Iqbal, We owe it to Anika to attend her wedding."

"You're right."

"Where's the invite? Go ahead and book us a hotel in Mumbai for the night of the thirtieth. Set up transportation for you and me. We'll aim to return the following day."

"Very well. Where is the venue for the wedding?"

"I have no idea," Raj considers for the first time.

"Check the invitation. It is somewhere in the stack of mail on your desk. Look around where you left it," Ram Iqbal instructs. The brother reaches his hand into the black hole of papers and picks out the wedding envelope. He then flings it towards Raj.

The invitation lands on Raj's lap. The boss puts on his glasses and opens the letter again. Out drops a folded note. Raj bends down, picks it up, unfolds it, and he notices that it is in Anika's handwriting:

"Raj, it's not too late. Call me. [Heart] Anika."

Adrenaline courses through Raj's body in an instant. He jumps out of his chair as if a dozen bees stung him at once. Raj is now standing with attention, wide awake. But he is unsure how to proceed. The boss takes another look at the invitation. "Ram Iqbal! The wedding is on the thirteenth, not the thirtieth! What day is today?" Raj looks towards his brother in shock.

Ram Iqbal looks grave. "Raj, today is the thirteenth."

Raj leaps into the air. "The wedding's today? I promised Anika I would attend her *mangala sutra* ceremony. Brother! We. Must. Go. Right. Now!"

Ram Iqbal replies with awe as Raj snaps out of his stupor for the first time in weeks. "You got it! Shall I arrange a flight?"

Raj looks at his watch. "No time. We must hit the road right away. Grab my pants and shirt and meet me outside in the car. We'll plan the trip once we're on the road."

"Sounds like a plan."

The Dancing Crows

Raj has a few options to make it to the wedding ceremony in time for the *mangala sutra* and *sindoor* ceremony. Even so, he decides to drive the whole way. So now Ram Iqbal and Raj are in the car. The vehicle once belonged to Raj's father, so it is beyond its years. The jalopy is useful for short trips around town, but it is the best they have for the moment. The brothers race through town in the dilapidated vehicle as they head towards Mumbai as fast as they can. But in the city limits, it is challenging to go faster than a jogging pace. The ground is wet, so there are puddles everywhere. And the streets of this part of Goa are not always paved.

"Raj, why don't we hire a driver? That way we won't get lost, and we can rest and be fresh for when we arrive."

"That might work. But how long is this drive anyway?"

Ram Iqbal is unsure and shrugs. "I estimate eight hours."

Raj thinks for a split second and then continues. The boss's mind is practical and sharp, but his heart is too optimistic. "That leaves us exactly enough time to make it, assuming we don't hit any traffic."

"Then maybe I should arrange a driver for us. The roads are filled with mountains and bridges, and you don't want to get lost either."

"No time. We can't waste even a second. We'll alternate driving."

It is clear that Raj's mind is focused on Anika. As the car speeds along, Raj considers to himself how the young lady will look in her traditional wedding dress. But he does not see a smile on her face. His heart fills with sorrow, and he thinks to himself, "Will she even be happy with this marriage?" His lungs let out a deep breath and the car presses onward towards the wedding.

Back in Mumbai, the Malhotra household brims with a whirlwind of excitement. The wedding is moving forward in full force. The family is busy with last-minute preparations.

As guests continue to arrive, others are enjoying a mid-day feast in the backyard. Prakash has a grand tent set up there to accommodate all the guests. Ramla and his expanded team have been cooking non-stop for the last three days, and they lay out the buffet lunch. Mangla has decorated the entire estate, inside and out, with fresh flowers. The fountain is alive with the energy of a careless toddler, bouncing water with might and vigour. Festive music blares throughout the compound.

The bride's father wears a sparkling white *sherwani*. It is dazzling with its intricate designs, and it glistens in the sun. He stands in front of the fountain, and he greets guests before they enter the house.

Meanwhile, Anika is in her room. "He looks like a disco ball," the daughter thinks to herself, looking down from her bedroom window. The bride sees the stream of guests entering the home below. She has never felt so alone as she does at this moment. Her eyes are swollen, but she does her best to hold back the tears. The young lady wears a dark red *sari* with gold borders. The dress that she picked out is elegant but not overly ornate as compared to her father's beaming attire. As she continues to look out of the window, her eyes penetrate the horizon. And her thoughts are buried in concentration as she tries to look into the heart of the city in the distance.

The bride then puts her hands together and gives a prayer to the heavens. And as she does, the young lady notices the crows dancing from tree to tree in the courtyard below. The birds play in the morning sun as if they have not a care in the world. And for some reason, for the moment, this gives her solace in her solitude.

The Compromise

It is now afternoon, and everyone is eager for the wedding to begin. The *baraat* ceremony will start soon, which is when the groom will arrive with his family.

There are signs of fanfare and merriment everywhere. Everywhere except upstairs in Anika's room. Prakash knocks on her door. He has come to wish his daughter well for the last time. As the father enters the room, he sees her still in front of her dressing table. She stares at herself in the mirror with a sullen expression on her face.

"Don't you worry." The father begins in an endearing voice, "You're going to look beautiful. Everything will be perfect and according to plan."

"Whose plan would that be?" the bride responds with a muted expression.

Prakash feels a hint of sorrow from his daughter. "Anika, dear... I know this wedding is not exactly as you had foreseen, but do understand that all I want is the best for you. I've tried to make this occasion as joyous as possible. We have magnificent and lavish decorations. I've planned grand meals. There is non-stop live music. And we have guests from all over. All this excitement and festivity is just for you."

Anika remains sad and sceptical. "Thank you, Daddy. I know you've tried your best."

"Well then, why the sadness, dear?"

She pauses for a second. "It's just that..."

"It's just what, dear?" The father rests his hands on her shoulders as he stands behind the daughter looking into her eyes in the mirror.

"It's just that this live *band baja*," the bride motions to the loud music radiating from the window. "And the celebrations," she then points downstairs. "And the *baraat* ceremony," she now looks towards the city in the distance. Anika pauses for a moment, and she peers far out into the sky, "All these things, they are here for a few days only."

Her eyes begin to swell with tears, "And I'm sure we'll all enjoy them very much." She is unable to control herself at this point, and she begins to sniffle in an effort not to bawl. She pauses for a moment and clears the wetness from her eyes with a tissue from her nightstand. The father stands with patience, waiting for the daughter to finish her sentence.

After another pause, Anika continues, "But for me, what is most important is something else. It is to spend my life with someone who will love and respect me for life. And there are only a few people that are lucky enough to get that. Everything else feels like a compromise."

Prakash responds, almost without thinking. "Anika, when this is all said and done, I assure you of one thing. You will have everything you need to have a happy, loving marriage and a secure and safe family."

"What makes you so sure?"

"I know, dear. Ask your mother. What else have I done for her and you but provide for everything that you both could ever need to be happy?"

Anika realizes that she is not getting anywhere with her father. They are speaking the same language, but their words are flowing past each other's heads. With some reservations, the bride capitulates, "You're right, Daddy. I'll be happy today, I assure you." She then stands to finish getting ready.

The father holds his arms out wide. "That's a good girl. Here, give me one final hug."

The bride moves into his arms. "Okay, Daddy."

The two hug each other. The patriarch wears an expression of pride and confidence. But the daughter is full of sadness and trepidation.

The Wall

The *baraat* procession makes its way down the street in front of the house. There is a live band with trumpets and drums. And with the music, there is dancing and jumping and cheering and yelling. The kids light off fireworks. Rahul sits at the centre of the celebration, high up on a horse.

The groom looks uncomfortable as if he is about to fall off with each passing step. And for this reason, the groom does not smile much. Rahul is out of his element, but nobody else in the *baraat* seems to notice as a veil covers his face. The groom's wedding party continues its slow progression towards the house.

From the house, many of the bride's guests are interested to see what the groom looks like, as they peer out the windows of the house. But the family's domestic servants feign indifference. Ramu wears a sombre frown as he goes about his business. He knows very well where Anika's heart lies, but he feels incapacitated to do anything about the situation.

Upstairs, Anika sits at her bedroom window. She looks out at the approaching *baraat* ceremony. And she comments to herself, "Rahul looks how I feel."

From inside her bedroom, the bride hears someone knock on her door. It is Sughandha, who calls out from the other side, "Ready, Anika?"

Anika turns towards the door. As Sughandha sticks her head in, Anika looks back at her with a lonely expression on her face.

"I'm to escort you down now," the woman whispers through the cracked door.

"Can't we just run away? Sughandha, sneak me out of here, and we'll make a run for the border."

The woman moves inside the room and closes the door behind her. "There are no borders, dear. Borders only exist in your mind."

Anika cannot believe she is having an actual conversation with Sughandha. But the betrothed does not understand what her escort is trying to tell her. "Of course, there are borders. Just look at that big wall surrounding this house."

Sughandha does not respond at first. But after a pause, she speaks up, "My husband hides behind his characters and impersonations. So that not even he knows who he is. But for me, I can escape to any place in the universe. All I have to do is open a book. And I'm free to disappear wherever I want to go."

"Yes, but I don't want to read my life away. I want to visit, see, and experience life full-on."

"Sometimes, life puts up walls that seem insurmountable. Only the ones that truly want what's on the other side will make it over."

Anika thinks this over but is not sure how to respond.

"So, dear, do you really want what's on the other side?"

Having never considered her situation in this way, the bride is not sure of herself. "I think so."

"Well, then go get it. Nothing is stopping you but the walls that you create in your head."

But the young lady still feels trapped in her current predicament. She has never taken a step this bold in her life before. And the thought of making such a drastic move shakes her to the core. "But I don't know how."

"If it's that important to you, I assure you, you do. For every problem, there are infinite solutions. Now come on, dear, everyone is waiting for you."

The Sindoor

Raj and Ram Iqbal bump along in the old car. The rusty vehicle churns and chugs along the highway at a steady pace. But it jumps and jerks every few seconds, for no apparent reason other than it is beyond its years.

The boss drives while Ram Iqbal navigates from the passenger seat. The travellers have almost reached Mumbai, so they are not too far from the wedding. Yet, Raj drives like a maniac as they weave through traffic. He knows that every second will count, so he does everything in his power to shave off time.

Meanwhile, the groom's procession has reached the *mandap*, where the wedding will take place. The magnificent structure is a raised platform with four pillars. And it has three pillow cushions for seats in the middle of it. Also, there is a small fire in the centre, along with all the necessary items for the day's final ceremonies.

The *mandap* rests under the far end of the backyard tent, and red rose-laden garlands cover every inch of it. All the guests have gathered under the tent. They all sit in eager anticipation of the ceremony, which will begin at any moment. The bride's family sits on the left, and the groom's sits on the right.

The priest kneels with pestilence, and the groom, seated on the cushion to his left, follows along. The ceremony initiates as the live band begins to play a romantic sonata. Everyone now stands in anticipation. They all look towards the house, where the backyard door is wide open, but there is no one there. The music plays on, and everyone is silent, and they look on with intent and zeal in their hearts.

Meena stands next to the *mandap*, and she searches for her daughter to appear. But the daughter does not. The mother looks back and forth between the door to the house and her future son-in-law's face a few times. And the music plays on. The mother's face is full of worry and angst. But this is nothing new, as she has felt this way all day. "It's just my nerves. Everything will be perfect," she tells herself. And the music plays on.

Ramla and Mangla stand by the backdoor to the home. The husband is to the left of the entrance. And the wife stands to the right. They look inside the living room from where they stand, but they both cannot see anyone approaching. So rather than cause others to worry, they both decide together to look directly into each other's eyes. And they smile at each other as if nothing were wrong. But in secret, they both hope that the bride shows up soon.

Ramu then makes an appearance from inside the home. Upon seeing him appear, the couple guarding the door breathes a sigh of relief. And so does everyone else. Ramu is calm and composed, and he walks up to the stage with style and confidence.

The trusty servant begins to address the guests, "Welcome, family and friends! We are glad you could make it today. And we will begin very soon."

No one is sure what to expect, but they are eager for the ceremony to begin. Even Meena looks on with anticipation, as she has no idea why Ramu is on the stage of the *mandap*.

And she also does not know why he is speaking right now. But she gives him the benefit of the doubt.

Ramu builds even more suspense by standing motionless for about a minute. He keeps his hands to his side, and his eyes closed. But he stands straight at attention. And then after a long pause, Ramu finally calls out, "Ladies and gentlemen, I present you the bride."

Anika appears in the doorway soon after. But upon seeing the bride, the entire room lets out a deep breath, in unison. Excitement is quick to radiate from the silent guests that are now standing and looking on. The live band begins to play again, and in an instant, everyone becomes sentimental.

The bride looks beautiful and enchanting. Her long veil stretches behind her, and she is majestic and lovely as she paces forward, one small step at a time. Prakash is by her side, and he locks his arm with his daughter's. And he does his best to hold back tears, but it is of no use. Both daughter and father feel very emotional. But it is not clear to the guests that they are so for entirely different reasons.

The bride takes her seat on the pillow next to the priest, and the priest begins with an invocation to the gods. And after this, the priest summons Prakash to the *mandap*.

The *kanyadaan* ceremony commences, where Prakash takes Anika's hand and places it on Rahul's. And in doing so, Rahul accepts Anika's hand into his own. Tears begin to spill down the father's face, as he feels illustrious and sincere at the same time.

The priest begins to recite the *kamasukta*:

> Who offered this maiden? To whom is she offered?
>
> Kama (the God of love) gave her to me that I may love her.
>
> Love is the giver, love is the acceptor

***

The hymn conveys the deep trust that the father is bestowing upon his new son-in-law. Prakash knows that no man will ever be good enough for his daughter. But in knowing this, the father still hopes that Rahul will care for Anika with all his heart. It is an emotional and sentiment-laden ritual. And by its end, both father and daughter are overcome with sadness.

The priest then initiates the *mangala sutra* ceremony. During this ritual, the groom ties a necklace around the bride's neck. And the beaded jewellery symbolizes the wife's devotion to her husband's wellbeing. Rahul takes the *mangala sutra* from the priest, and he ties it around the bride's neck with care.

During this process, the groom begins to notice that his bride does not look well. He places his hand on Anika's arm and pulls her body closer to himself. He leans into her ear, and whispers in a calm but concerned tone, "Are you okay? You look nervous."

Rahul wishes to know what is going through his bride's mind. But even without knowing, he can tell that something is not quite right. Before the wedding, the groom solicited advice from his mother a few times. "Don't you think I should get to know my future bride more than this?" he asked her soon after the engagement. "We only met a few times. I don't even know her favourite colour or her favourite animal."

The mother's reply was warm, but not comforting, "So you won't marry her because she likes blue and not purple? Plus, that is not our custom, my son. You know this. My dear, you have the rest of your life to uncover all your bride's mysteries, passions, and secrets. Why the rush?"

This conversation did little to comfort Rahul at the time. And as he relives his mother's words in his mind right now, the groom cannot help but feel that something is off. "Brides will be nervous. I get that. But I see nervousness with my patients all the time. This is different," he thinks to himself.

Anika whispers back, her voice shaking, "Yes. I guess I am."

Sensing that something is wrong, the groom turns towards the priest. "Let's hold off on the *sindoor*; we can apply the vermillion later, in private."

The priest nods back in compliance. "As you wish." He puts down the tub of the orange-red cosmetic powder used for the *sindoor*, and he moves on with the ceremony.

The Stray

The brothers are now in the city of Mumbai. There is traffic everywhere as it is mid-day and the city is alive with clamour and excitement.

Raj's driving is as reckless as ever, and Ram Iqbal holds on for his dear life. "Raj, we want to arrive in one piece, you know."

Before the driver can reply, the car speeds into a crowded intersection a few seconds after the light turns red. The jalopy comes inches away from sideswiping another truck carrying old tires. The truck driver swerves and breaks in time, but old tires fly off the back and spill all over the street behind them. Raj almost loses control of his vehicle but manages to keep it on the road and in one piece.

"SLOW DOWN!" Ram Iqbal screams this time.

At the next intersection, Raj encounters even more chaos. This time he must swerve to avoid killing a medium-sized stray crossing the street. Rather than run over the canine, the boss oversteers to the left. But then he has to steer back to the right to avoid hitting a *pav baji* vendor.

This causes the dilapidated vehicle to lurch out of control. The jalopy darts to the opposite side of the street and crashes head-on into a pole. Raj is not wearing a seatbelt, and so he ejects from the car. His body lands face-down on an oncoming vehicle, and he shatters the windshield.

Ram Iqbal, who is wearing a seatbelt, looks rattled up but is safe in the passenger seat. Traffic comes to a standstill around the scene. The mutt approaches Raj's mangled body and begins to lick his fingers. Raj's fingers begin to give a faint movement in response to the dog, but beyond this, his body lies motionless.

The *pav baji* vendor runs across with his hands in the air. The dog goes over to him and lies down by his legs. It becomes clear that the two know each other, as the dog gives its friend a knowing look. The vendor walks over to Ram Iqbal and opens his car door. Ram Iqbal unbuckles his seatbelt and takes the vendor's hand as he climbs out of the totalled vehicle.

"Don't try to move your friend," the vendor instructs. "There's a chance they can still save him. I've already called an ambulance."

Ram Iqbal looks mangled, and he nods in agreement as they both begin to pace towards Raj's body.

"Crazy dog," the vendor continues. "That's the second accident this month she's caused."

At his feet, Ram Iqbal notices Raj's cellphone on the ground, laying a few feet in front of Raj's mangled body. Ram Iqbal picks up the phone, finds Prakash's phone number, and calls him.

Back at home, the father has just finished his part of the *kanyadaan* ceremony. Prakash now walks away from the *mandap* and towards the house, so that he can wipe the tears from his eyes. He did not expect to become so emotional from the ceremony, so he wanted a few moments to regain his composure.

As Prakash enters the living room, his phone begins to vibrate. The father sees that it is Raj calling, and so he answers the call. "Raj, I know why you're calling. Now listen..."

Ram Iqbal says something to Prakash, who is now silent. The father listens with sincerity after hearing the tone in Ram Iqbal's voice. Prakash's face turns white as he hangs up the phone. He now has a grave expression across his countenance. The father steps back outside and runs towards the *mandap*. He puts up both of his hands above his shoulders and yells, "STOP!"

At once, everything comes to a halt. Everyone turns towards the father, who wears a grim expression across his face. "A man is about to die. I owe this man my life. I must help him."

Upon hearing this, Anika immediately understands that this is Raj. She stands up and stares straight into her father's eyes. She carries a look of extreme fear and horror in her own eyes. But Parkash's expression does little to mitigate her panic. "This cannot be happening!" the bride screams to herself.

The Patient

Prakash runs through the double doors of the emergency room entrance of the hospital. Not far behind is Anika, Meena, Ramu, Sughandha, Ramla, Mangla. And behind them is pretty much the entire wedding procession.

A nurse runs up to Prakash and gives him the latest on Raj. "Dr. Malhotra, the patient is in critical condition. We've sent him straight to the operating room. The patient has lost lots of blood. He has fractured more than half of his ribs. And he has internal bleeding from his upper gastric area. We had to intubate him."

"Thank you, Nurse," the doctor responds. "Prepare the fluids and five hundred CCs of B positive. I'll begin operating right away."

The Zap

Raj is in critical condition. The doctors and nurses are doing their best to keep him alive. Prakash rushes into the room and he begins to wash his hands in haste. As he is soaping up his hands, the surgeon takes a swift look at this friend on the table. At that moment, Prakash recalls the oath that he made to his friend. He recalls telling Raj that he would repay him one day for saving his life. "This is the day, my friend. I won't let you die on me," the surgeon whispers to himself as he approaches the operating table.

Prakash begins the surgery without haste. But the surgeon is quick to realize that the situation looks grim. Raj's heartbeat is unstable, and the internal bleeding is now slowing down.

Ram Iqbal is in the waiting room by himself as the wedding party begins to fill up the empty space. The brother, bandaged with a minor injury on his elbow and brow, spots the bride from the crowd. He steps up to her, and before he can say anything, the bride sees the look on his face, and she collapses into his arms. They both let out an agonizing cry in unison. And they embrace each other as if they are family, although they have never met before.

Everyone is nervous and unsure of the outcome. "The patient has not yet stabilized, and that is all the update we can give for now," says the nurse as she speeds away. This update does little to ease the fears of everyone. All they can do is wait for another update. Anika cannot keep herself together. And she bawls her eyes out as she leans into her mother's comforting embrace.

In the operation theatre, Raj is still bleeding profusely. Prakash is stitching as fast as he can, but the damage is severe. Prakash's hands begin to shake. The nurse beside him notices, and inquires, "Doctor, shall we call for extra help?"

"No! I can do this. I just need to stop the bleeding." Prakash barks back.

The nurse concedes and hands him another layer of gauze. But the bleeding continues and the surgeon becomes even more flustered. Prakash then calls out without looking up, "Nurse! Get me Dr. Banerjee. And we'll need a specialist from cardiology."

The nurse responds, "Right away, Doctor." The nurse rushes away from the operating room to carry out Prakash's orders.

The surgeon gets more nervous, as nothing will stabilize the patient. Soon after, the EKG machine flatlines. The body goes under cardiac arrest. "Nurse, defibrillator. Now!" he yells.

Before the paddles can charge all the way, the surgeon places the nodes on the patient and yells, "Clear!" Prakash sends a zap through his friend's body. And then one more, "Clear!" And another zap. And again a few more times. But nothing seems to work. Raj's lifeless body lies there motionless. Devastation fills Prakash's heart. All the doctor can do at this point is to put his head down in despair and cry into his bloody hands.

The Vermillion

Prakash comes out of the operating room, his gown covered in his friend's blood. As he steps down the hallway, past the emergency room, and towards the waiting room, his feet begin to wobble. His vision begins to blur. And his whole body begins to shake without control.

Many thoughts race through Prakash's mind, but none of them make any sense. The only words that seem to mean anything to his brain are 'If only.' But these words come with nothing else and thus provide little solace. And so the doctor's entire being cannot make any sense of the situation he is in.

Even so, his legs move forward. And as the physician approaches the waiting room door, he takes a deep breath to steady his gait. But it is of no use. His being is overcome by grief and tragedy, and there is nothing he can do to regain composure. Still, the surgeon pushes forward through the doorway. And he enters the waiting room, where every awaiting eye snaps towards his direction. And it is in that instant where the doctor sees the last shred of hope vanish from everyone's face.

Prakash pauses for a few moments. And then the words "We lost him" spill from his lips. The doctor strains to keep upright, but there is nothing to lean against where he is standing. The bloodstains all over his gown provide enough details. Yet, the physician manages to utter three more words before losing it. "I lost him," the doctor groans towards the heavens. And his face falls into his hands as his knees bend and he begins to drop to the floor.

Upon hearing this, Anika collapses into her mother's arms. The bride wails with enough emotion to awake the sleeping moon. And her vision turns to black as she can no longer see past her eyes as her body presses deep into her mother's embrace.

Ramu goes up to Prakash to lift the man up before he collapses to the floor. And Ramla also helps steady the doctor to his feet. But both servants require all their strength to keep the physician steady.

Emotion drenches the room with despair. And before anyone can regain composure, two nurses roll the body into the area. The deceased lies in peace with a white sheet covering the body. Yet fresh blood continues to soak through the covering to his side and on top.

"Doctor, we need you to sign off of the body for transport," the nurse in front hands the surgeon a clipboard.

The father accepts and signs the letter on top and places the board on the gurney. "Move quickly, okay," he tells the nurse.

There is already an ambulance waiting outside. The nurse nods in compliance, and both nurses rush the body towards the exit.

"Daddy, where are they taking him?" Anika pleads with fear and torment in her voice.

Prakash turns to his daughter and puts his arm over her shoulder to console her. "They're transporting the body to the trauma centre. Raj was an organ donor. His body will save many lives."

The word 'body' echoes back into the young lady's ears. She recalls Raj's notion that one day her buddy will be just a body, and she cannot for the life of her believe that that day is today. Her heart swells with trepidation and remorse and her bones begin to shake and rattle under her skin. Anika sobs to herself, "My buddy is now a body. My buddy is no more." The anguish in her soul is unbearable.

As the gurney passes in front of the young lady, she calls out, with tears in her eyes, "Stop!"

The nurse that is wheeling the stretcher stops and looks at Anika. The bride moves over to the stretcher and uncovers the top half of the body. Raj is lying there in peace. Anika hugs him and says, "Raj, I'm so sorry. I'll never forget you. If there is one thing that I know, it is that you have changed me for the better. And I will always have you in my heart."

She buries her head on his shoulder and lets out a long wail. As she pulls her head away, some of Raj's blood is now smeared on her forehead.

Rahul, with his left arm around his mother, stands by the far wall of the waiting room. Both mother and son are dismayed, but also, they are sincerely saddened by the tragic passing of this man that they do not know.

"Raj must have been someone truly incredible," the groom thinks to himself. His eyes are full of grief, but his legs feel like stones cemented to the floor.

At this point, Rahul's mother steps away from her son and comes forward to the bride to consoler her. "I see the *sindoor* ceremony is now complete," the mother gives Anika a tender caress.

Confused, the young lady reaches up to her brow with her hand, and she wipes her forehead. She then looks down at her fingers and sees the blood smeared across them. Anika sniffles and then whispers back, "Yes, I guess so."

Rahul's mother continues, while she places her arm around Anika's shoulder and pulls the bride close to her body. "Dear, I want you to listen to me."

Anika turns towards Rahul's mother's face and looks into her eyes with intent. "Okay, I will," she whispers.

"This man before us must have been an incredible soul," the mother utters. "It's clear that he meant a great deal to many caring people," she gestures across the room with her free hand.

"Yes, he did," the young lady cries back.

"So please understand that I now speak from my heart."

Anika nods in compliance.

And after a pause, the old lady continues, "I don't want you to marry my son."

At first, this does not register to Anika. "I'm sorry." The bride peers into the mother's eyes. "I'm so sorry," the young lady shakes her head and tears well up in her eyes all over again.

"No, dear. Don't be sorry. Trust me. Rahul will be fine. There's no need to spoil your life in marrying my son. We all need to find our own peace. But I know when something is not meant to be when I see it. And I see it here today. Your peace will come in time. I assure you of this. So do not worry, my dear."

Anika puts her hands together and bows with respect. "Thank you."

Rahul's mother leans forward and takes the *mangala sutra* off from around Anika's neck. "Dear, the true sign of a Hindu bride is the *sindoor*, the red vermillion." She points to Anika's forehead. "The rest, including this *mangala sutra*, is for fashion," she points to the necklace in her palm.

The young lady looks into her the mother's eyes and nods in agreement and sincere appreciation.

At this point, Meena comes over and gives her daughter a big, comforting hug, "It's okay, dear. Everything will be okay."

The Mourning After

Two days later, the Malhotra family is back in their home in New Mumbai. The entire house feels sombre, and everyone is in mourning. The father, mother, and daughter gather on the couch. They all wear white colours, as is customary when someone in the family passes away. And everyone is overcome with sadness.

The phone next to the couch rings and Prakash picks up. "Malhotra residence."

The person on the other end speaks, and after a few moments, Prakash responds with, "Thank you, Ram Iqbal."

The father hangs up and then turns towards Meena and Anika. "The funeral will be in Goa. Ram Iqbal has already booked tickets and accommodation for everyone."

"Everyone?" Meena inquires.

"Everyone. Ramu and Mangla, get everyone ready and pack your bags. We're all going to Goa."

The Salute

The Malhotra family arrives at the airport in Goa the next day. It is tiny as there is only one terminal, so they do not have to travel far before they reach the passenger pickup area.

And as the party exits the terminal, they run into a train of three big, black vans in the passenger pickup area. Each vehicle has the logo "Raj Industries" on the side door. And each one has a tuxedo-wearing chauffeur waiting by an open door, ready to help and assist the family.

Prakash steps up to the first van, and the driver gives him a warm greeting. "Welcome to Goa, Doctor. From all of us at Raj Industries, we wholeheartedly welcome you and your family."

"Thank you very much, sir." The father gives the driver a stern but thankful nod and proceeds to enter the van.

Ramu walks up to the driver of the second van, and before he can say anything, the driver gives Ramu a confident salute. Ramu salutes back and nods in appreciation.

The rest of the family piles into the two vehicles in front. And the drivers load the baggage into the third. The three vans then exit the airport, one after the other in an orderly fashion.

The Tip

The hotel lobby is expansive and lavish but decorated with an elegant, but simple décor. All the furniture is black wicker, but the pieces appear to be expensive in nature. The entryway boasts a grand vaulted ceiling with extensive timber supports. The floor is pink marble, which matches the colour of the vests of each staff member. At the far end, the vast space opens out into the beach, where the palm trees keep a watchful eye on the blue ocean beyond the shore.

The family enters the space after unloading from the transportation drop off area. And everyone regathers in the lobby of the hotel. Prakash steps up to the check-in counter, "Allow me to speak with the manager."

The receptionist, a young lady, no older than his daughter, greets the father. "Good afternoon, Doctor Malhotra. Is everything okay?" she inquires.

"I would like to speak with someone in charge," the doctor demands, with a stern expression on his face.

"I am more than happy to check everyone in. We have everyone's rooms all prepared for you and your family," the receptionist replies.

Prakash shakes his head as if there has been an enormous mistake. "No, you don't understand. My entire family is here. And for some reason every time I go to pay for something, nobody accepts my money. What kind of operation is this?"

The young lady is unsure how to respond, but she does her best to ease the man's concerns. "Sir, you do not need to pay anything with us, I assure you. RI has everything covered."

"Raj Industries owns this hotel?" Prakash opens his mouth all the way, his face showing complete disbelief.

"Yes, sir. As you know, RI is very big in the hospitality industry."

Prakash pauses for a moment and begins to speak. Too many thoughts race through his head, so he is not sure where to begin. Even so, the father shakes his head again, as if to force coherent thoughts into his mind. He then speaks up with added worry in his voice, "But this is business. How can you make any money if you don't charge us for anything? The transportation, the restaurant we all ate at, these rooms... nobody will allow us to pay for anything. I've noticed the same with all the guests here. The waiter at lunch even returned my tip. What exactly is going on?"

"Sir, we are in mourning for our founder. And it is no secret that we are all here working for free. We are here out of respect for our beloved boss. May he rest in peace. So there's no need to pay for anything. Everything is taken care of, I assure you."

The father is more than confounded by this entire conversation. And so his brain tries to parse one point at a time rather than everything all at once. "Very well. But..."

He then looks around the lobby from where he stands, and then the father examines the face of the woman. He thinks that by searching her face, he might uncover something that her words cannot reveal. But soon Prakash gives up. And he continues his questioning, "But who orchestrated all this? Who exactly is in charge of this operation?"

"Sir, Mr. Ram Iqbal has arranged everything. You do not need to worry. In fact, he has left you this note."

Prakash takes the note from the concierge and reads it to himself. "Dear Dr. Malhotra, I have arranged for everything. You do not need to worry. I will see you this evening. The driver will take you and your family to the Raj's residence after you settle into your rooms."

Upon finishing the note, Prakash looks back up at the concierge.

The concierge gives a simple reply as if she can read his mind, "Mr. Ram Iqbal will see you this evening. The driver will take you and your family to the main residence when you are ready."

Prakash gets the impression that he will not get any more information out of the young lady. So all he can do at this point is to nod back in agreement. "Very well. We'll be ready in one hour."

The concierge calls the doorman. "Kartik, kindly prepare the vans for the Malhotra family in an hour."

"Very well, sir," the doorman replies, turning towards the patriarch. "Right this way, sir. I'll take you to your rooms," Kartik motions to Prakash and the family.

The White Kurta

The residence is a large estate spread over a dozen acres. There is a tall, see-through fence surrounding the compound, with a metal gate in the centre that faces the road. And on the entrance are two big bronze letters, 'RI' And behind the fence, upon a hill, sits a grand mansion.

And as the family pulls up to the gate, they see that thousands of people have already gathered outside. The crowd is there to pay last respects. While they mourn Raj's death, they also celebrate his life. Some are holding signs, such as, "Raj is king" and "Raj Industries Forever." Many are crying. Hundreds of mourners hold candles up in the air. And there is sadness everywhere. But at the same time, the situation is extraordinary. Music blares from all directions, and there is fanfare all around. As Anika looks out of the van, she considers to herself, "I can't believe how many people this man affected. I know my life would have been completely different without Raj. But the same must be true for all these people."

The young lady is in awe, but at the same time, her heart pounds with angst and longing. She does not know how she will face Ram Iqbal. She knows in her heart that she did not cause Raj's death, but a part of her still feels guilty for his passing. Her brain fills with thoughts that begin with 'If only,' but her mind struggles to finish the sentence. The best she can conclude is that perhaps she should not have sent Raj her wedding invitation. "After all, if Raj never received the invite, he would not have been in the accident." And it takes Anika considerable strength to come to terms with this understanding.

The grand estate is colonial in appearance. It boasts a large masonry facade that is ocean blue. And each window has two large non-functioning shutters on each side, the colour of lime green. Up the long driveway, there are tall poplars on each side in equal proportion and spacing. Where the pavement ends, so begins the finely laid stone carport, as large as a half a cricket field. And at its centre is a fountain. But this fountain's basin is no smaller than a moat that would surround a castle. And within this mini-lake there are jets shooting water high up in the air, higher than the house, it seems. And behind the home hides the ocean in all its vastness.

As the family pulls up to the courtyard, Ram Iqbal steps out from the entrance of the home. He walks out to greet the family as they unload themselves from the vehicles. "Now this would put the Bellagio to shame," Prakash thinks to himself as he steps down from the transportation.

First, Ram Iqbal walks up to the father, as Meena and Anika step up next to Prakash. The brother extends his hand to the father, and after taking his hand, Ram Iqbal steps in to give the doctor a hug. "So glad you could make it, Prakash."

"Thank you, Ram Iqbal."

Ram Iqbal then turns towards the mother. "Meena, have you rested up?"

"Yes. You've taken such good care of us, Ram Iqbal. Thank you so much."

The brother gives her a sincere embrace.

Ram Iqbal then turns towards Anika, and before he can say anything, she gives him a big hug. The young lady folds herself into the brother's arms and loses all composure. "Ram Iqbal, I'm so sorry." She breaks down and almost falls to her knees, but Ram Iqbal keeps her on her feet, as she begins to sob.

The brother consoles her. "No apologies needed, my dear. I understand how you feel. Everything will be okay in due time. Trust me. It will get better."

Anika cannot stop herself from crying. "But he was such a good man. It's all my fault."

"There is no fault here," Ram Iqbal affirms. "I need you to understand this, Anika." He pulls her back from his embrace and looks into her eyes. "I assure you, you only made his life better. We will all miss him. But we will never forget him either."

Anika nods in agreement. "Thank you, Ram Iqbal."

The brother now turns towards the family. "Come this way, the body is in the centre of the rotunda, towards the back of the house." As the party begins to walk towards the entrance of the home, Ram Iqbal fills them in a bit. There are people everywhere, as they are all eager to pay their respects to the body.

"We are allowing a few hundred people in at a time. Everyone is welcome. But we want to make sure everyone gets the time they need with our dearest Raj before his body must move on. As you may know, Raj is the wealthiest businessman in these parts. He had over two thousand employees across three dozen businesses in Goa alone. In one way or another, Raj has affected all these people you see here today. But his legacy will never be forgotten for generations."

The interior of the home is straightforward, even though the house itself is quite large. Ram Iqbal continues his monologue as the party makes its way through the house. "Raj was well-off, of course, but he believed in simplicity. In fact, this residence was only used for business dealings and corporate events. It was once the home of a wealthy British lord. But since independence, this estate fell into disarray. And the property lay abandoned, wasting away. Nobody wanted to deal with the massive upkeep involved. And the title had too many outstanding loans on it. A real nightmare. So the estate was all but forgotten to time."

As the guests follow Ram Iqbal through the home, they encounter many colonial-style paintings, statues, and sculptures. The artwork seems old, but everything is well kept. And in front of each piece, there is a descriptive plaque.

The family enters a large hall, where countless mourners wait to see the body. And Ram Iqbal continues his speech from the doorway to the room, "Not long ago, Raj purchased this home. And his goal was to turn it into a museum one day. And one day, I'm sure we well. But this is where we will begin this evening's vigil. I hope you all will attend." The grand hall has a thirty-foot ceiling. And intricate tapestries cover the left and right walls, which do not contain windows. But there are many windows on the far wall, which looks out into the deep blue sea.

Ram Iqbal explains, "Raj's actual home, where he spent most of his time, was his cottage by the water near your hotel. And the RI corporate headquarters is near the downtown. That is where our management team handles the day-to-day operations. We'll head there tomorrow to take care of some business."

The party then begins walking down a long hallway filled with people, young and old. "Raj built a kindergarten, with free tuition for all his employees. But he didn't stop there. He then built a secondary school. And then a university. Again, the family of employees can attend for free. But he didn't stop there. Raj then built a hospital, two museums, and three parks. We are all forever grateful for his never-ending philanthropy. Raj cared for his fellow human beings, irrespective of age, status, and gender. He was a simple but great man."

The party now enters the rotunda in the backyard of the home, where Raj lays on a large white table in the centre. He wears a simple, white *kurta*, with no other embellishments. And he appears to be at peace. Upon entering, and upon seeing the body, Anika's legs begin to falter. But she steadies herself against her mother's side. "Be strong my girl, I am always here for you," Meena gives her daughter's hand a firm embrace.

Anika looks into her mother's eyes and tears well up enough to consume her vision. The mother wipes them away with her free hand, and whispers into her ear, "It's okay. Be strong for Raj."

The young lady takes a deep breath. She then frees herself from her Meena's shoulder, and she takes a few paces towards Raj. But Anika's legs soon turn into bricks. Unable to move, she stands there alone, looking at the body. And in that instant, the young lady's mind begins to scream in torment. Her hysterical thoughts, full of contempt, rage, and sorrow, are loud enough to wake the sleeping moon. But her body is silent. The young lady feels like she is about to drown as her mouth fills with invisible water. Panic consumes her body, and her legs begin to melt onto the floor.

As gravity begins to take over, an arm catches Anika's weight mid-fall. The large hand pulls her up towards his massive body. Like a bear saving its cub from running over a cliff, Prakash holds his daughter tight to his chest. Anika closes her eyes, and she gasps for air. "Breathe, my girl. Breathe! You can do it." But Anika's soul is deep within her mind, locked away, like a treasure within a bank vault.

"I'm so sorry. I'm so sorry. I'm so sorry. I only wanted the best for you, my girl. But I see the pain that my ego has caused in those I love the most in the world. Please know, I never meant for any of this. But I know if there is anyone to blame for your suffering, it is me. And me alone." The father pleads to the daughter's ear, with her body rigid in his arms.

The daughter's mouth opens wide. She finally takes a deep breath of air. It is as if she is coming up for air after sinking deep into a salty, black sea. She sucks oxygen deep into her soul, but then she begins to hyperventilate. Even so, the embrace of the father begins to penetrate her consciousness. Her shaking soon begins to steady in his powerful arms. The young lady regains her composure after some time. Then she takes another deep breath. But this one is more voluntary as compared to the previous. The daughter stands on her feet. She frees herself from her father, with more resolve this time. And Anika whispers to her father as she steps forward towards the dead body, "Thank you, Daddy."

The father sets her free. The young lady continues to meander forward again, both arms crossed over her chest. Her body shivers, and so Anika scratches her elbows for comfort. "Please give me the strength to face this man that I love," she pleads to the heavens above as she takes one small step at a time.

When she reaches Raj, at last, Anika bends down and touches his feet out of respect and love. Her eye sheds a single tear as her face meets his. But she forces herself to look him straight on, knowing this will be the last time that she will ever see his face again. "I will be strong for you, my Raj," the young lady whispers out loud before she turns back around.

The Body

Later that evening, and after the vigil, everyone gathers on the front lawn of the estate. The casket now rests upon an open-air cremation site. And the crowd gathers around it in a large circle. The entire compound swells with an enormous gathering of people from all over the town, state, and country.

The site itself is a circular platform raised above the ground with cement blocks. And on its centre rests the casket. Wooden logs surround it as if a small child were building a fort with the wooden box in the centre as its foundation. And to the side of the platform is an altar, where a small fire flickers on top.

The sky is clear, and the night is warm, and the moon shines from above, filling the air with a dull glow. But the flame from the alter also gives a solemn mood to the evening. And no one speaks, as well. Except every now and then, someone else cries out in vain to the heavens above. But for the most part, muffled sniffles fill the air.

The thousands of individuals that Raj touched over his life swarm the roads. And the streets outside the gates continue to fill with crowds of folks. Ram Iqbal steps up to the altar, and he performs the final rites. The brother then takes a log, lights it on the flame, and places the wood next to the others by the casket. And as he does this, the brother cries for the first time since Raj's death.

The other logs are quick to ignite, and in less than a minute, the entire platform fills with a tremendous blaze. Soon after this, the crowd disperses into the night. As everyone is walking away, Anika approaches the altar to say her final farewell.

The young lady approaches the cremated body, pauses for a moment, and puts her bent arms on her hips. "Listen body, you weren't supposed to leave me so soon."

She pauses for another moment to control her rapid breathing. "But I now see you've accomplished more than I could imagine in your short time on this planet. Raj, I'm so humbled. You are a caring soul. I will ensure that no matter how long I live, I will work my hardest every day to continue your legacy. You devoted your life to charity and giving. I see that now, and I wish the same for me. I want you to know that I've also decided to never marry. Rather, you've shown me that there's more to this world than the ties of marriage. I understand now that I have too much to give. Too much to do. I pray for all the strength I can get to follow a short distance in your footsteps. Goodbye, good friend. I love you, and I will miss you. But I will never forget you."

The News

The next day, a single black van enters the expansive Raj Industries headquarters. The complex is modern and vast. There are about a dozen buildings, each with a similar style. And a series of bicycle paths connect each structure. In front of each building, there are about a dozen bicycles parked in front. Each bike is of the same make and model and colour (green). Inside the vehicle, Prakash, Meena, and Anika sit in the backseats. And the chauffeur is by himself up front.

The driver gives the family a quick tour of the complex as he drives to the main building. "Raj began building this complex about ten years ago. In the beginning, he operated out of his cottage. He did that for over a decade. Then we moved to his bigger estate. The one you saw yesterday. After that, he started to build and expand this development."

"He must have been working non-stop," Prakash observes in awe.

"Yes, for sure," the driver responds. "I've never seen him take even a day off. And I've known him for over twenty years."

"Wow, not even one day?" Meena questions.

The driver nods and gives a confident reply, "That's right, even weekends. In fact, it was big news around here when Raj took a few weeks off for the first time last year. It even made our local paper. At first, none of us believed him. Then one day Raj got up and left Goa and disappeared for over a month. They said it was for some type of reunion or something. Who knows!"

Upon hearing this, Meena and Anika look at Prakash, and they are all astonished to comprehend all this. The van pulls to a stop, and the family steps down from the vehicle. "I'll be right here when you're ready," says the chauffeur who waves from the driver seat. And the three guests make their way into the central building.

The Snack

The secretary guides the family through the office. She is an old lady in her late sixties, but she is thin and fit. And although she is wearing a traditional sari, she wears neon blue sneakers on her feet.

The woman reminds Anika of Mangla, and the young lady wonders how she and the others are doing back at the hotel. This is the first time everyone from home has travelled this far together. But Anika was glad to hear this morning that the rest of the household planned to spend the day on the beach. "A welcome break, for sure. There's nothing you haven't thought of is there, Raj?" the young lady whispers this to herself as she follows the secretary onto the elevator.

They step off on the top floor of the ten-story building. The secretary guides the family into the boardroom at the far end of the penthouse floor. "Please have a seat here. May I offer you anything to drink?" the old lady asks.

"Water please," says Prakash as he pulls out a chair for Meena and another for Anika. All three of them take a seat. The room has a massive, singular window pain that overlooks the complex below. Every now and then, an employee on a bicycle darts from one building to another. It is party-cloudy but still sunny, and in the distance, the ocean waves make a calming appearance.

The secretary pours three glasses of water from a large crystal jug placed on the centre of the mahogany table. She returns the pitcher back so that it now rests next to a bowl of snacks on the long table. She then puts one glass in front of each visitor. "I'll notify Mr. Jain of your arrival. Help yourself to some snacks," the old lady suggests as she exits the room and closes the door behind her.

In the room, on the far wall, hangs a large portrait of Raj. He has a garland of fresh flowers tied around it. Upon seeing the picture, Anika bows her head and gives a small prayer. She hopes that his soul is in peace, and at the same time, she considers how young he looks in the painting. "It's as if his body was meant to live forever. But maybe his soul had more pressing matters to attend to up there," Anika wonders to herself.

And a few minutes later, Ram Iqbal in jeans and a black t-shirt and a middle-aged gentleman in a suit enter the room. The family stands up to greet them.

The brother begins. "I'm glad you all could make it before heading back today. This is Mr. Jain."

"Thank you, Ram Iqbal," Meena replies. "You've been so kind."

Mr. Jain greets the visitors. "My name is Taran Jain. I am Raj's personal attorney. Thank you for coming." He then shakes Prakash's hand. "Dr. Malhotra. Pleased to meet you. Please have a seat."

Mr. Jain walks over to the mother and shakes her hand. "Meena Malhotra. Come over here and have a seat." He then turns towards the daughter. "Anika Malhotra. Thank you for making it here today. Do sit down."

"What is this about, Mr. Jain?" the father speaks out. "Do you know why we're here today?"

Everyone takes a seat, and the attorney opens a folder that he has placed in front of himself. As he does so, he declares, "I do. Let me explain. I would like to take a moment and review a few things with you. So I appreciate your coming down here. And thank you again for your time today. I know hanging out in an office building is the last place where you want to be right now."

"Very well," Prakash responds. "So, what is this all about?"

The lawyer continues. "I have had the pleasure of working for Raj and Raj Industries for over two decades. More than anyone else that I know, this man understood that life is about the journey, not the destination. Yet, Raj lived a simple life. He believed in simple living, but with high thinking. He could have lived a lavish lifestyle, yet he lived modestly. However, Raj chose to live this way because of who he was as a person, as you may guess by now. Even so, Raj understood that not everyone has that choice. And he did not think it right that where you end up depends so much on where you begin. Especially because most people do not begin so well as he did. That is not to say he had an easy life. We all know that his mother abandoned the family when he was too young to remember. And that his father left him a failing business when Raj should have been in school. But true knowledge is knowing that which you can control, and that which you cannot. And wisdom is working on the former while accepting the latter."

Mr. Jain becomes emotional while speaking all this. So he takes a moment to regain composure before continuing. "Raj told me this the day I started working for him. And I'll never forget it, as I will never forget him. So above all, helping those in need gave my boss the most satisfaction in life. And this is what drove Raj to create all that you see around you."

The family nods back in uncertain anticipation. "I see this now," Prakash responds. "I must say, I did fail to truly understand my dearest friend. I wish I had known him better."

"Perhaps, but you did know him. Indeed, he never had any grand ambitions. Or grand plans. And he didn't do all this to leave a legacy to his greatness. He could care less about all these things, as I'm sure you know," Ram Iqbal admits. "Rather, there is no big mystery to my brother's life. He simply lived each day as best he could. No more. No less. And in his work, he saw the opportunity to help those around him. And so he did. From his point of view, he just felt that he was lucky enough to do so."

"Nevertheless," Mr. Jain explains, "Raj's wealth qualifies as an empire. Whether he wanted one or not is inconsequential. And with his passing, we want to ensure his life's work continues as he would have wished if he was alive and with us today."

The family is not sure what to make of all this. So after a pause, Meena inquires, "But Mr. Jain, what does this have to do with us? We're happy to help out in any way, but what could you possibly want from the three of us?"

The lawyer puts the tips of his fingers together and pauses for a moment. "That's why we're all gathered here today, to review Raj's last will and testament. He updated it only last month. And I'm sure you'll all want to know about what it says."

Mr. Jain pulls out the first sheet from the folder and begins to read. "On behalf of my estate, I do hereby formally bequeath thirty-three percent of my assets to Ram Iqbal. To my dearest brother, you may not live forever, but clearly, you have outlived me. Nobody knows my wishes better than you. I know you do not plan on retiring anytime soon, if ever. So I leave you with more work than you can imagine."

Everyone turns towards the brother. And Ram Iqbal looks at the portrait hanging on the wall. He stares in the eyes of his brother, and gives a confident reply, "It would be an honour, my brother."

The lawyer pauses for a moment to clear his throat. He stands up to pour himself some water from the jug on the table. And he takes a long sip before sitting down again. Anika could not be prouder of Ram Iqbal. "Raj, there is only one person on this planet that could fill your shoes. And you're so lucky that he is your brother," the young lady whispers to the painting. Her cheeks begin to glow with happiness. A feeling that she has not felt in a long time.

Mr. Jain pulls out the next page from his file, and he continues to read out loud. "Next, I hereby bequeath another thirty-three percent to a trust. This trust will oversee all my foundations and charities. This includes the medical clinic and the senior citizens' home. It also includes the school for the blind, the library, the parks, and the nursery school. And most important, it includes our orphanage for our disadvantaged children."

"This trust will be managed by Meena Malhotra. For this role, the organization will compensate her twenty lakhs a year, adjusting for inflation each year, for as long as she is able."

This astonishes the entire family, but Meena most of all. The mother's face turns red, and she is not sure what to make of the proposal. She is about to faint, but Prakash steadies his wife by placing his hand on her thigh. Anika turns towards her mother, and the daughter screams with excitement. "Mommy, can you believe it?"

"I don't know what to say," Meena cries out.

"Trust me, you'll be a natural. If there is one thing that Raj knows how to do well, it is to pick the right people for the right job. I've admired this in him more than any other quality. He didn't always know the right answers to a situation. But he always picked the right people who could figure it out." Mr. Jain assures the mother with a healthy level of conviction in his voice.

The wife looks into her husband's eyes and sees the young man that she once knew when they first met. His eyes are full of passion and admiration at the same time. Meena turns to face the lawyer and shouts out to the room, "I accept!"

And everyone cheers. "Meena, I cannot tell you how impressed Raj was with your coordination skills. We will do great things, I assure you." Ram Iqbal reaches across the table to shake her hand. And she responds with a confident grip and a mile-wide smile.

The attorney then reads the next paragraph. "As a first project, the foundation will commission three temples. One in Goa, another in Mumbai, and another in the city of the project lead's choice. Funds for this project will be more than sufficient. But each temple must be built so that it can feed at least five thousand each day. The project lead for this grand undertaking will be Doctor Prakash Malhotra." Mr. Jain places the sheet on the table and looks at the father in the eye.

The father is speechless. His eyes begin to swell up, but he maintains his bearing. Never in his life has the doctor been so proud of someone else as he is now of his childhood friend. "Raj, you are an endless bag of surprises. And you are a better human than I can ever hope to be. But I assure you, I will devote the rest of my life to this. And I will not let you down, my dear friend."

Anika jumps from her chair upon hearing this. And she lunges forward and gives her father a big hug from behind his neck from where he sits. "Oh, Daddy, I love you so much."

She then places one arm around each seated parent and pulls their heads towards hers. "I just know in my heart that you'll both make Raj so proud."

The young lady is so giddy that she cannot contain herself. "Wow. Wow. Wow. Wow. Amazing!"

The lawyer clears his throat to grab the daughter's attention as he pulls out another page from the file. "There's still more."

Anika looks up and gives Mr. Jain a thumbs up, and she then retakes her seat.

After everyone settles down again, the attorney begins to read from this next page. "And finally," Mr. Jain declares, "I do **hereby** bequeath the remaining portion of my estate to Anika Malhotra. She will manage Raj Industries with the help of Ram Iqbal for as long as she is able. And she will ensure that our never-ending work can continue into the next generation and beyond. Every human deserves to live long and prosper, now and forever. And only with the help from each one of you will our mission succeed."

The family is genuinely taken aback, and Anika is speechless. The young lady stares straight into the lawyer's eyes as if she is waiting for him to shout "April fools!"

But all Anika can do in response to Mr. Jain's confident expression is her shake head in disbelief.

She then searches Ram Iqbal's face for answers, and so he responds back with two thumbs up, "You got this, Anika. I know you do."

But all she can do in response to this is resume shaking her head. "This can't be," she blurts out at last. A million thoughts race through her head, but most of them are too rapid to make any sense of them. The young lady's head becomes light. And her mind begins to go blank as she starts to feel faint. At that moment, she feels a hand on her thigh, which gives her leg a squeeze.

It is Prakash's hand, and he calls out to Anika's blank expression, "Anika. Anika, dear. This choice is yours, and yours alone. Whatever you decide, your mother and I support you one hundred percent. And no matter what decision you make, or no matter what happens, we will always love you."

After a moment, Anika takes a deep breath and a long sip of water. The daughter then looks towards the portrait with tears in her eyes. And she then looks back at the boardroom table with a sense of uncertainty and trepidation.

"Before we continue, I have something for you, Anika. It's a letter from Raj." Mr. Jain takes the envelope out from the folder and pushes it forward to Anika.

The young lady picks it up, tears it open, and unfolds the hand-written note inside. She then reads it to herself, "Dearest Anika: One day you will tell your story of how you've overcome what you're going through now, and it will become part of someone else's survival guide. You got this, Anika. I know you do. Much love, Raj."

Anika folds the note back up and places it back in the envelope. She then stares at the centre of the boardroom table with a blank expression on her face. Positioned there in the middle is a bowl full of peanuts and beans.

The young lady places a fixated stare at the snack, and after a few more deep breaths, Mr. Jain pushes the bowl towards Anika. "Go ahead, dear," the lawyer states, "have some. You know this was Raj's favourite, right?"

She pauses for a second as if recalling something. Then after a second later, Anika gives a thin smile as she takes a handful from the bowl. The young lady pops a peanut in her mouth as if she now has a renewed sense of purpose in her heart.

"There's one more paragraph," calls out the attorney. Mr. Jain takes the final page from the folder, and he clears his throat before reading it. "I know all this must seem daunting. There will be times when the world will come crashing down upon you. Yet, there is endless suffering in the world. And often charity comes at a great personal sacrifice."

Everyone is silent. And Prakash, Meena, Anika, and Ram Iqbal look at the lawyer with eager anticipation with what he is about to say next.

Mr. Jain now stands up and continues reading with the paper in his hand. "But know this. When you devote your life to something greater than yourself, magic happens. There will be days when your morning chai tastes like sunshine. Times when simple street music makes you dance on the spot. Complete strangers will make you smile without control. And the moon in the night sky will touch your soul. You will fall in love with being alive all over again. And your life will never be the same. But only if you live outside of your mind. And in your heart. The choice is yours. And yours alone. With gratitude, Chairman and CEO of Raj Industries, Raj."

These words take some time to filter through the room, so everyone takes their time to digest. Mr. Jain places the sheet down on the table, and he retakes his seat.

And now everyone turns their attention to Anika, and Ram Iqbal then solicits her directly. "Well Anika, do you accept this great challenge and responsibility?"

Anika pauses and then stands. She takes a deep breath. And she walks under the painting of Raj, looks up at him, and speaks to him as if he was standing in front of herself, "Yes, I do. Just for you."

The Epilogue

Early the following year, the Malhotra family relocates to Goa, and they settle into Raj's tiny cottage home, by the water. Meena assumes her position as head of the foundation. And Prakash retires from surgery to focus his efforts on the first of three temples.

Ramu embarks on a stand-up comedy career, with Sughandha has his agent. Mangla and Ramla open an internet café in downtown Mumbai, and they hire Dhansukh and his twin Mansukh to manage it. Rustom posts to Facebook a photo of his son and his wife. They both wear matching black t-shirts that say, "It's a girl."

And Anika begins the arduous task of assimilating into Raj's empire, under the astute guidance of Ram Iqbal.

Tolstoy takes up residence at Raj's palatial estate. Upon the very first directive of Meena and Anika, the sprawling estate is now an orphanage and retirement home combined into one. And in this home, the elderly take care of the children. Or is it the other way around? It is hard to tell sometimes.

THE END

CPSIA information can be obtained
at www.ICGtesting.com
Printed in the USA
BVHW040328121022
649231BV00023B/41